MAX STEEL™

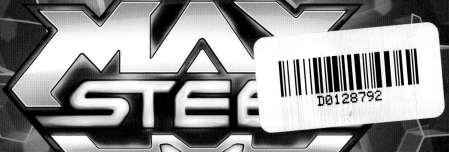

•HERO OVERLOAD•

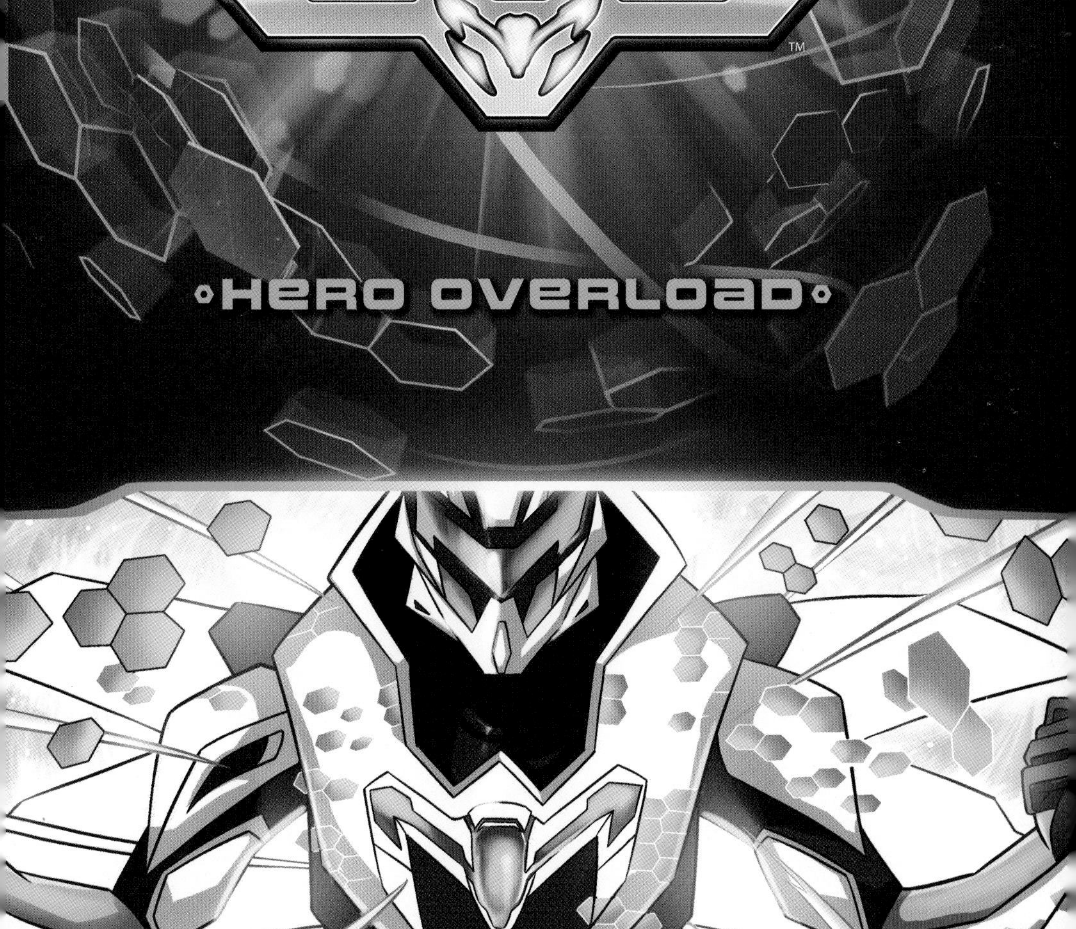

STORY BY
B. CLAY MOORE
ART BY

max steel™

Volume 2
Hero Overload

Story by B. Clay Moore
Cover Art by Albert Carreres
Cover Colors by Alejandro Torres
Interior Art by Alfa Robbi
Interior Colors by Burhan Arif
Letters by Zack Turner

Design/Sam Elzway
Editor/Joel Enos

Special thanks to Gabriel DeLaTorre, Lloyd Goldfine, Cindy Ledermann,
Michael Montalvo, Jocelyn Morgan, Julia Phelps and Darren Sander.

Printed in China

Published by VIZ Media, LLC
P.O. Box 77010
San Francisco, CA 94107

10 9 8 7 6 5 4 3 2 1
First printing, January 2014

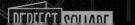

°HERO OVERLOAD°

TABLE OF CONTENTS

WHAT IF THE ULTIMATE SUPERPOWER CAME WITH A MIND OF ITS OWN?

To the world at large, turbocharged Max Steel is the newest, coolest, most beloved superhero. To the secret organization of N-Tek, he's their number one ally in the ongoing fight against mayhem, monsters and alien invasion. And to supervillains, he's the only source of Turbo Energy in the universe and therefore incredibly valuable and sought after—by

MAX & STEEL

Two heads are better than one, unless one belongs to a stubborn teenager and the other belongs to a headstrong alien. Somehow, these two have to learn to cooperate as one entity, superhero Max Steel, protector of the universe!

KIRBY

Max's best friend at school is always on the lookout for fun, adventure and hijinks.

SYDNEY

The girl Max likes is also one of his best friends. But super-heroics often ruin any attempt to take this friendship to the next level.

MOLLY

Max's mom is an ex-agent of N-Tek, the secret group that Max relies on for his high-tech support and guidance.

any means necessary. But really, he's just 16-year-old Maxwell McGrath, former regular guy, who's got a whole bunch of crazy new powers and now has to figure out how to live constantly connected (and sometimes merged) to N'Baro AksSteel X377, a wisecracking alien with an attitude who's not always the most cooperative partner. Together, these two friends from different worlds combine to make one superhero...and will have to figure out how to save the universe!

ワ-TEK

A highly secret, super-scientific organization that protects Earth from technological and biological threats. Founded twenty years ago by Forge Ferrus (now the head of N-Tek), Miles Dredd and Jim McGrath (Max's father), N-Tek and its agents use advanced alien technology to aid Max in his role as Earth's best hope from invasion.

BERTO   **KAT**   **FORGE**

VILLAINS

DREDD

The former co-founder of N-Tek went rogue after a heated argument resulted in an explosion and the disappearance of Max's father, Jim McGrath. Now fused with a Turbo Energy siphon into his own body, which he needs to fuse with Turbo Energy to stay alive, Dredd is constantly on the hunt for more Turbo—which is why he's after Max.

NAUGHT

Dredd's right-hand henchman has some diabolical designs of his own. He may seem like a nerd but he's still a formidable foe.

PROLOGUE: Fame

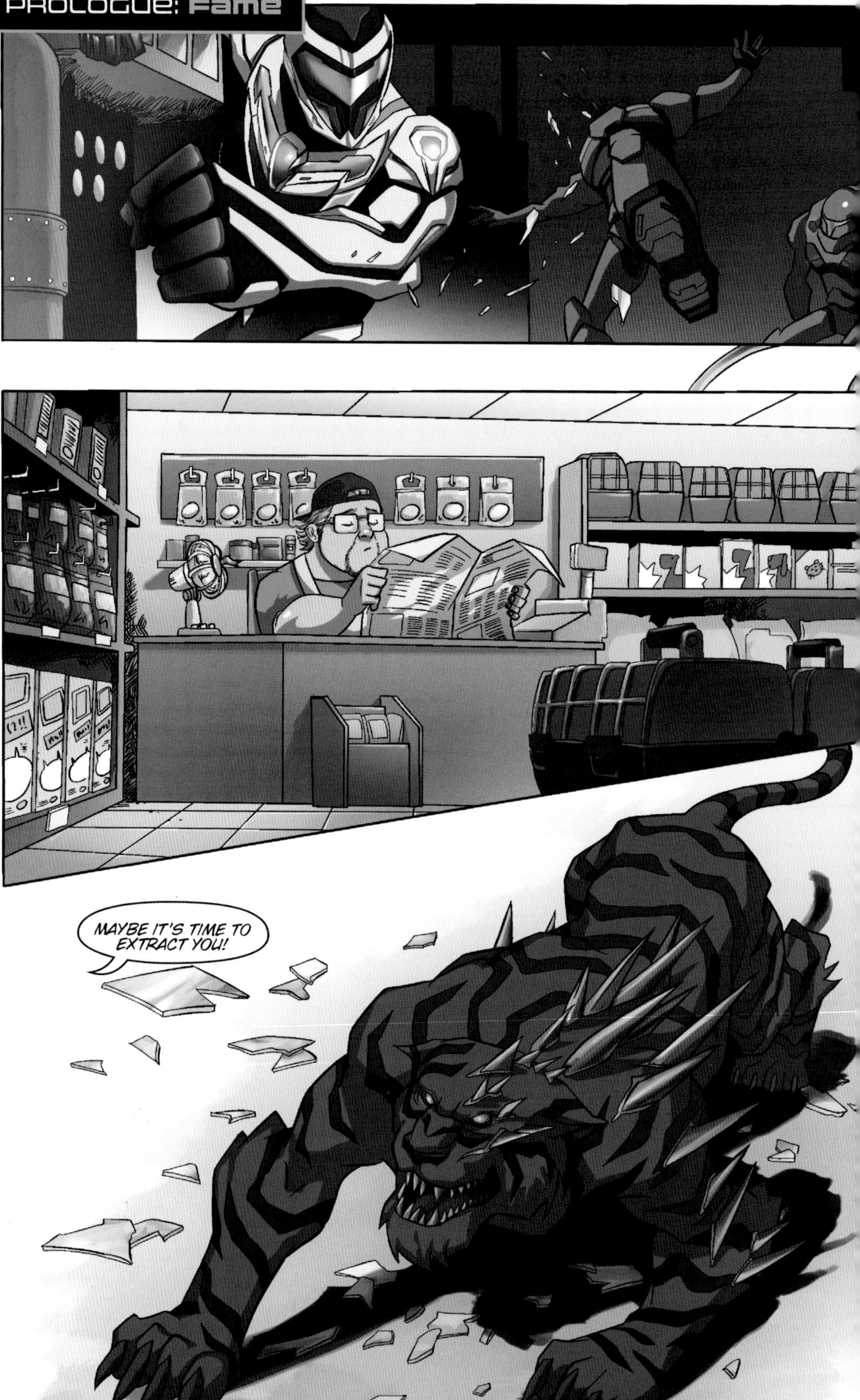
MAYBE IT'S TIME TO EXTRACT YOU!

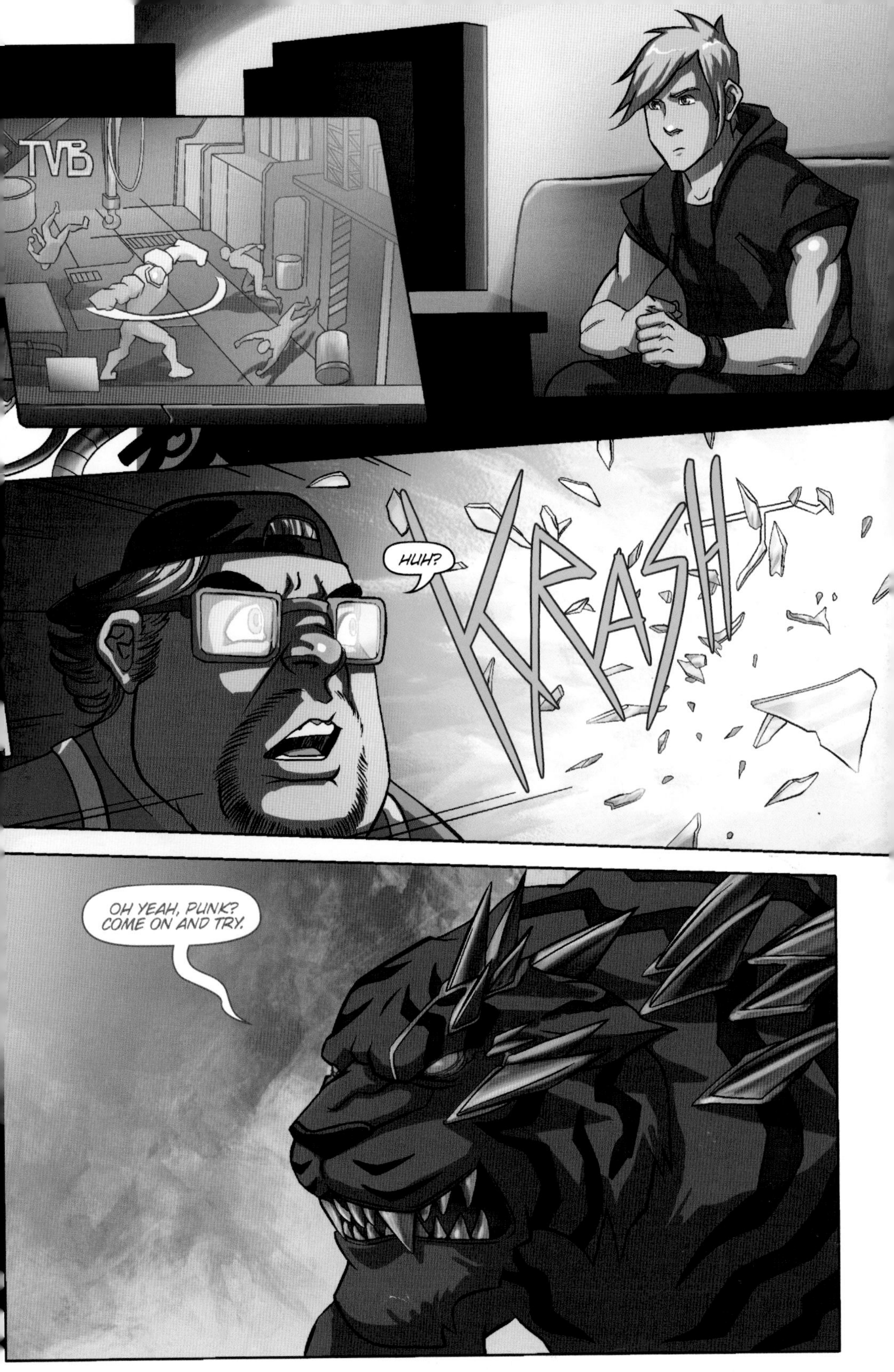
TVB
HUH?
KRASH
OH YEAH, PUNK? COME ON AND TRY.

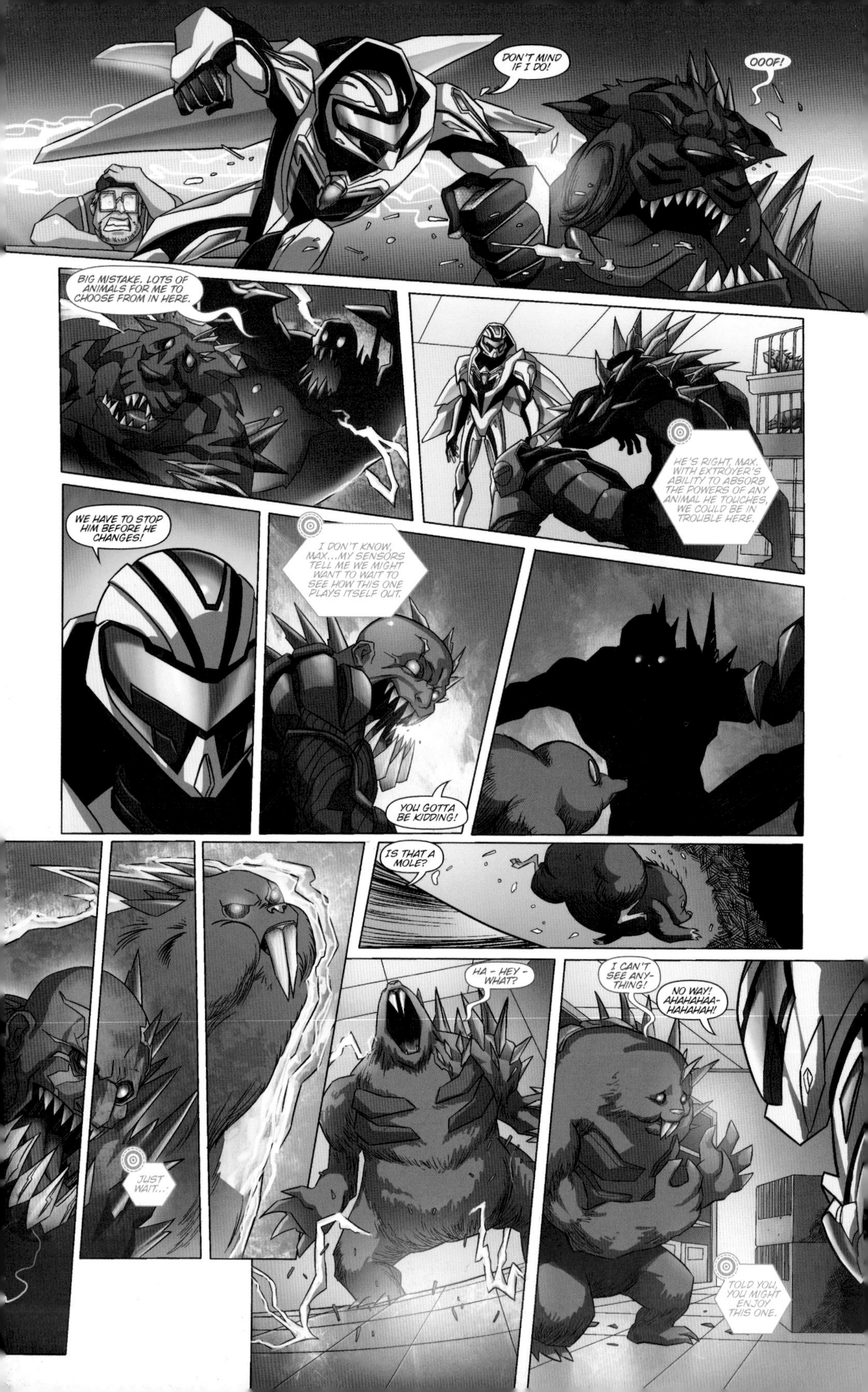

DON'T MIND IF I DO!
OOOF!
BIG MISTAKE. LOTS OF ANIMALS FOR ME TO CHOOSE FROM IN HERE.
HE'S RIGHT, MAX. WITH EXTROYER'S ABILITY TO ABSORB THE POWERS OF ANY ANIMAL HE TOUCHES, WE COULD BE IN TROUBLE HERE.
WE HAVE TO STOP HIM BEFORE HE CHANGES!
I DON'T KNOW, MAX... MY SENSORS TELL ME WE MIGHT WANT TO WAIT TO SEE HOW THIS ONE PLAYS ITSELF OUT.
YOU GOTTA BE KIDDING!
IS THAT A MOLE?
JUST WAIT...
HA - HEY - WHAT?
I CAN'T SEE ANY-THING!
NO WAY! AHAHAHAA-HAHAHAH!
TOLD YOU, YOU MIGHT ENJOY THIS ONE.

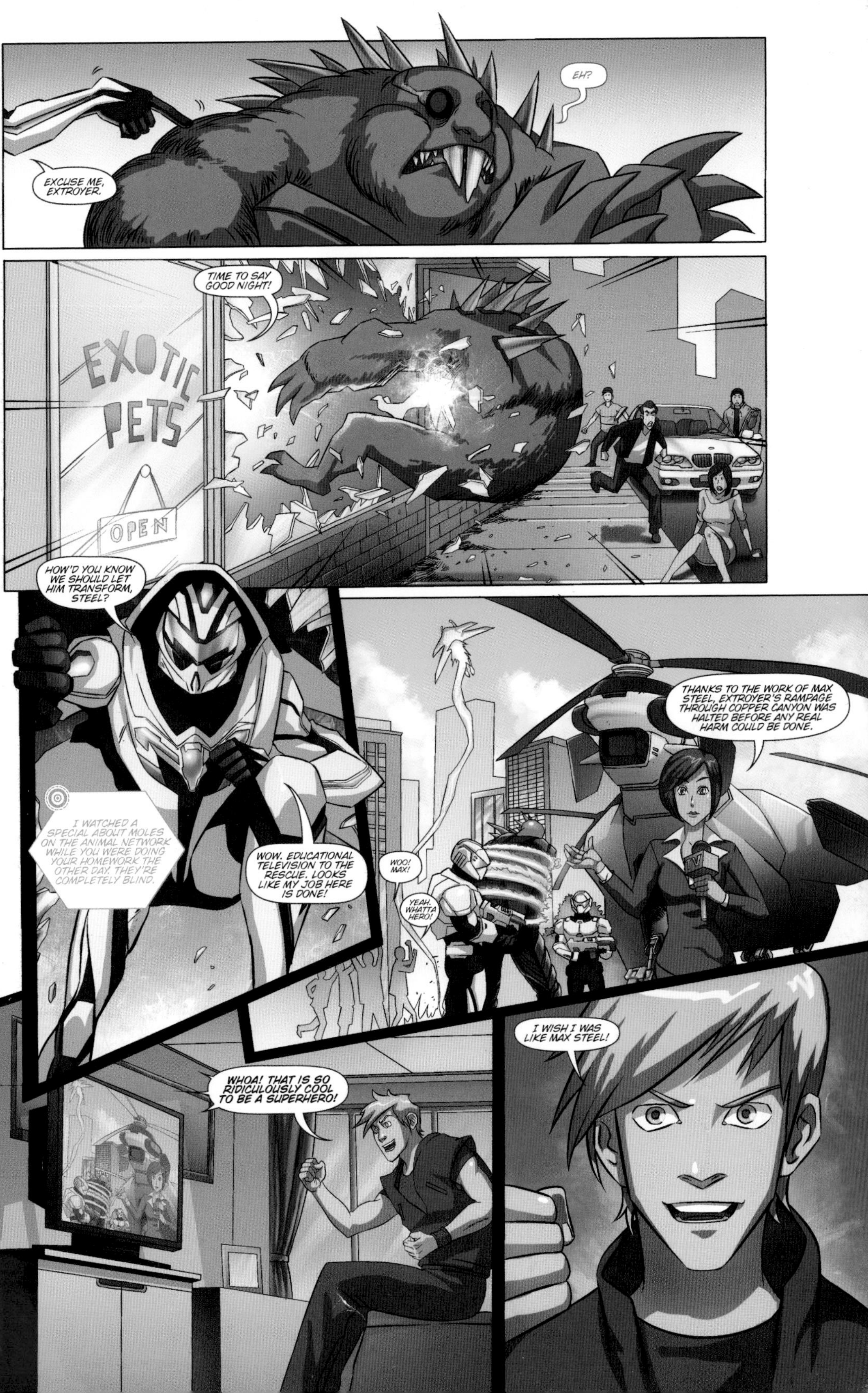
EH?
EXCUSE ME, EXTROYER.
TIME TO SAY GOOD NIGHT!
EXOTIC PETS
OPEN
HOW'D YOU KNOW WE SHOULD LET HIM TRANSFORM, STEEL?
I WATCHED A SPECIAL ABOUT MOLES ON THE ANIMAL NETWORK WHILE YOU WERE DOING YOUR HOMEWORK THE OTHER DAY. THEY'RE COMPLETELY BLIND.
WOW. EDUCATIONAL TELEVISION TO THE RESCUE. LOOKS LIKE MY JOB HERE IS DONE!
THANKS TO THE WORK OF MAX STEEL, EXTROYER'S RAMPAGE THROUGH COPPER CANYON WAS HALTED BEFORE ANY REAL HARM COULD BE DONE.
WOO! MAX!
YEAH. WHATTA HERO!
TV
WHOA! THAT IS SO RIDICULOUSLY COOL TO BE A SUPERHERO!
I WISH I WAS LIKE MAX STEEL!

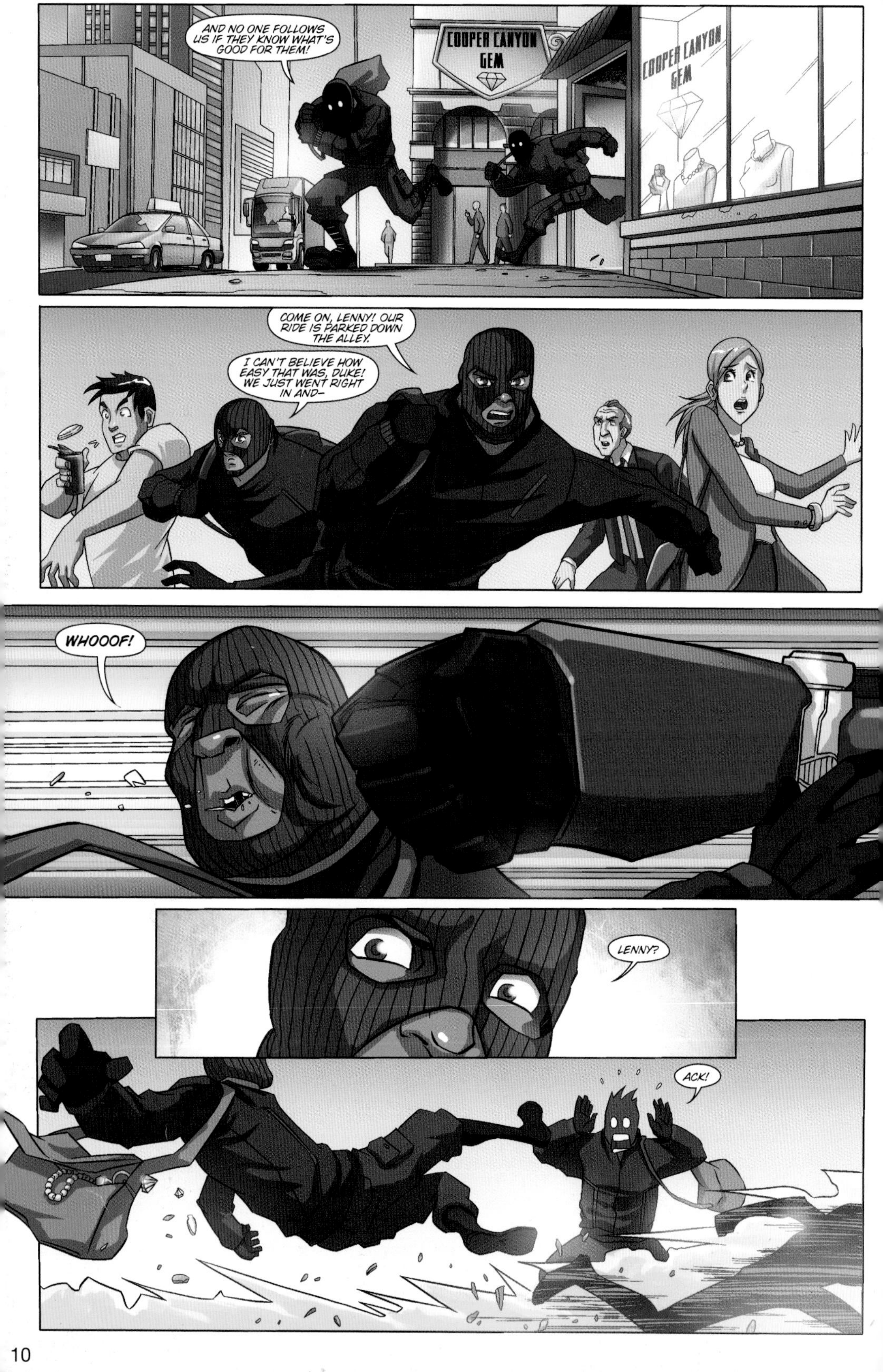
COOPER CANYON
GEM
COOPER CANYON
GEM
AND NO ONE FOLLOWS US IF THEY KNOW WHAT'S GOOD FOR THEM!
I CAN'T BELIEVE HOW EASY THAT WAS, DUKE! WE JUST WENT RIGHT IN AND–
COME ON, LENNY! OUR RIDE IS PARKED DOWN THE ALLEY.
WHOOOF!
LENNY?
ACK!

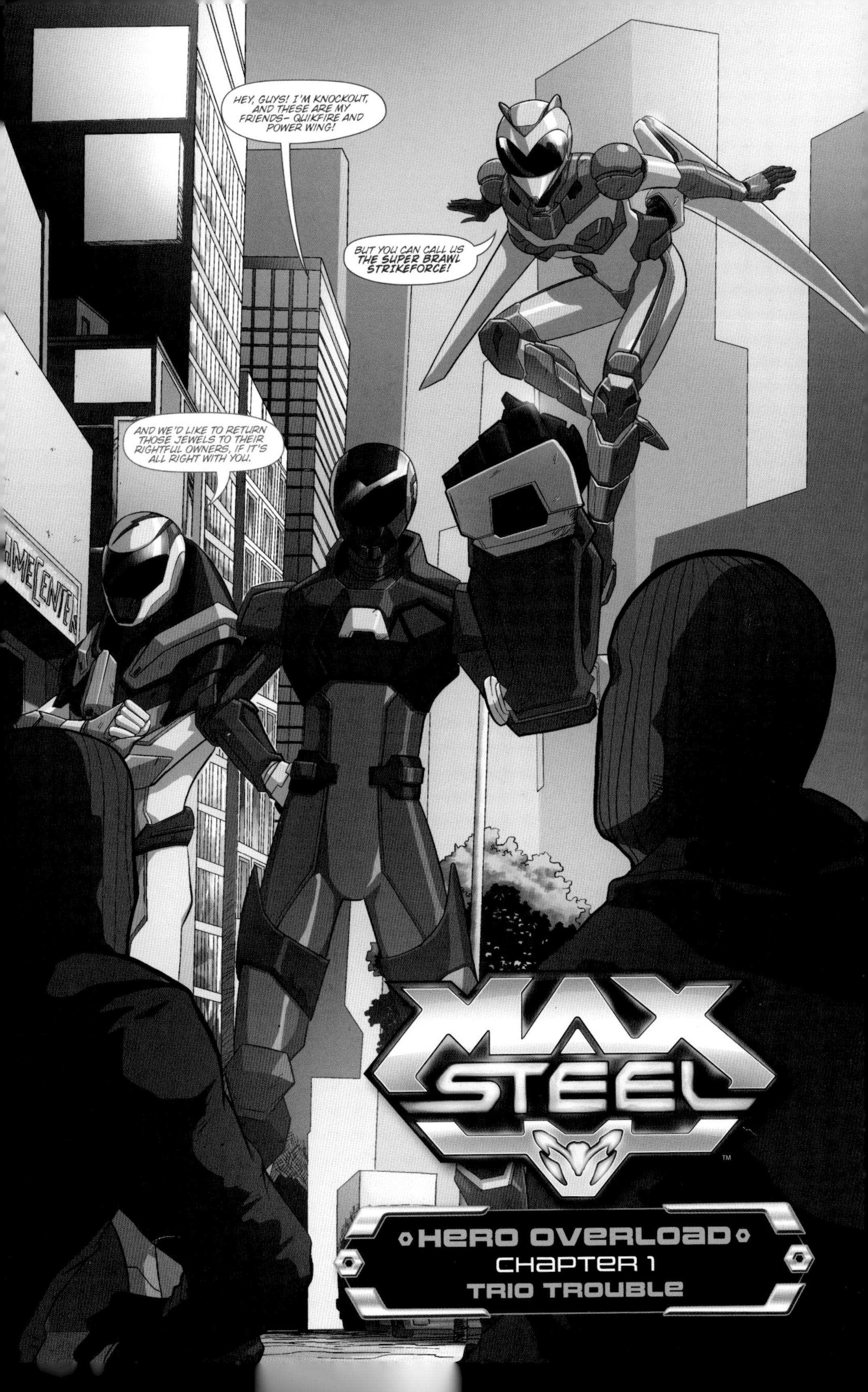
HEY, GUYS! I'M KNOCKOUT, AND THESE ARE MY FRIENDS- QUIKFIRE AND POWER WING!
BUT YOU CAN CALL US THE SUPER BRAWL STRIKEFORCE!
AND WE'D LIKE TO RETURN THOSE JEWELS TO THEIR RIGHTFUL OWNERS, IF IT'S ALL RIGHT WITH YOU.
MAX STEEL
HERO OVERLOAD
CHAPTER 1
TRIO TROUBLE

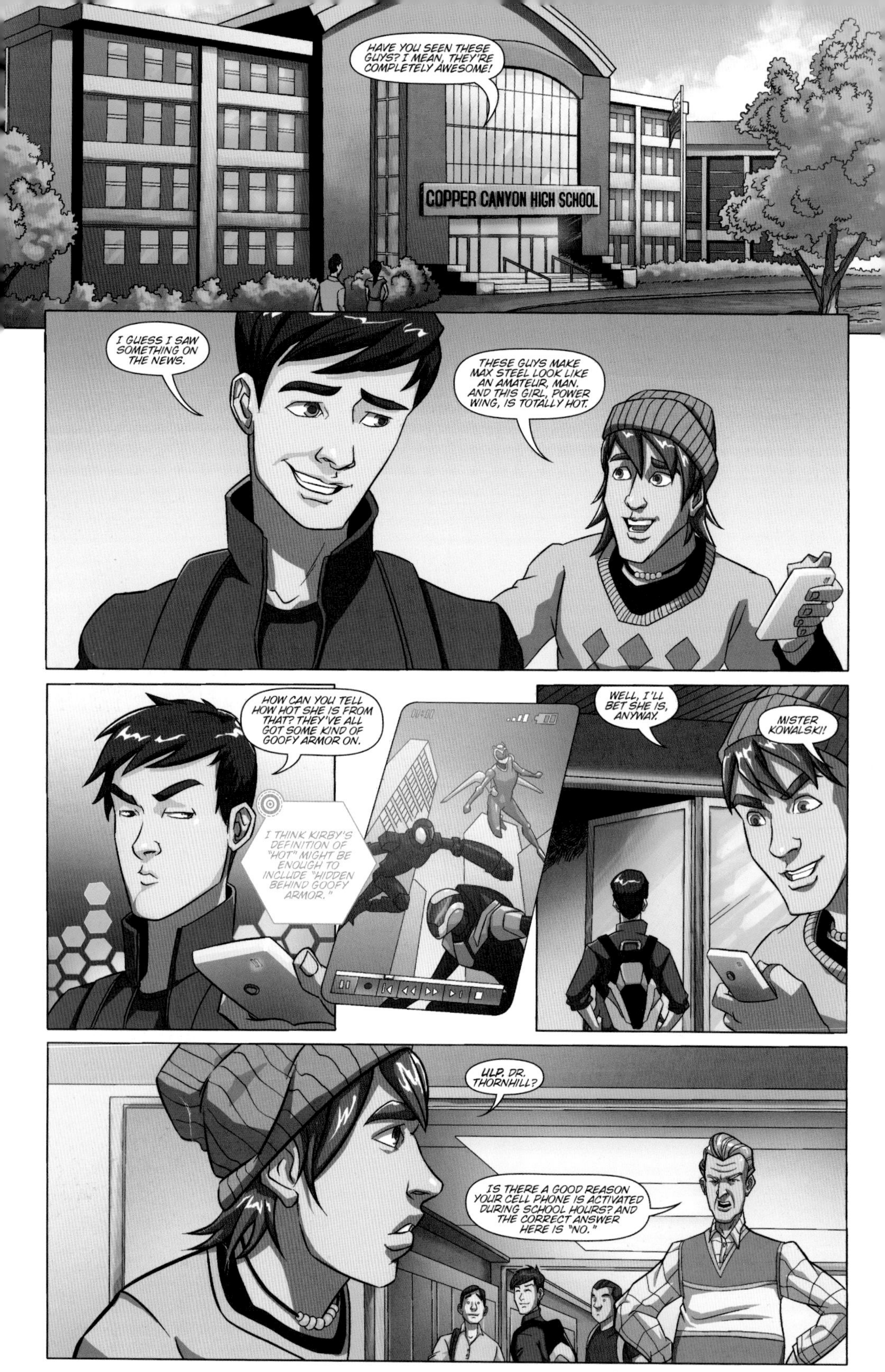
HAVE YOU SEEN THESE GUYS? I MEAN, THEY'RE COMPLETELY AWESOME!
COPPER CANYON HIGH SCHOOL
I GUESS I SAW SOMETHING ON THE NEWS.
THESE GUYS MAKE MAX STEEL LOOK LIKE AN AMATEUR, MAN. AND THIS GIRL, POWER WING, IS TOTALLY HOT.
HOW CAN YOU TELL HOW HOT SHE IS FROM THAT? THEY'VE ALL GOT SOME KIND OF GOOFY ARMOR ON.
I THINK KIRBY'S DEFINITION OF "HOT" MIGHT BE ENOUGH TO INCLUDE "HIDDEN BEHIND GOOFY ARMOR."
WELL, I'LL BET SHE IS, ANYWAY.
MISTER KOWALSKI!
ULP. DR. THORNHILL?
IS THERE A GOOD REASON YOUR CELL PHONE IS ACTIVATED DURING SCHOOL HOURS? AND THE CORRECT ANSWER HERE IS "NO."

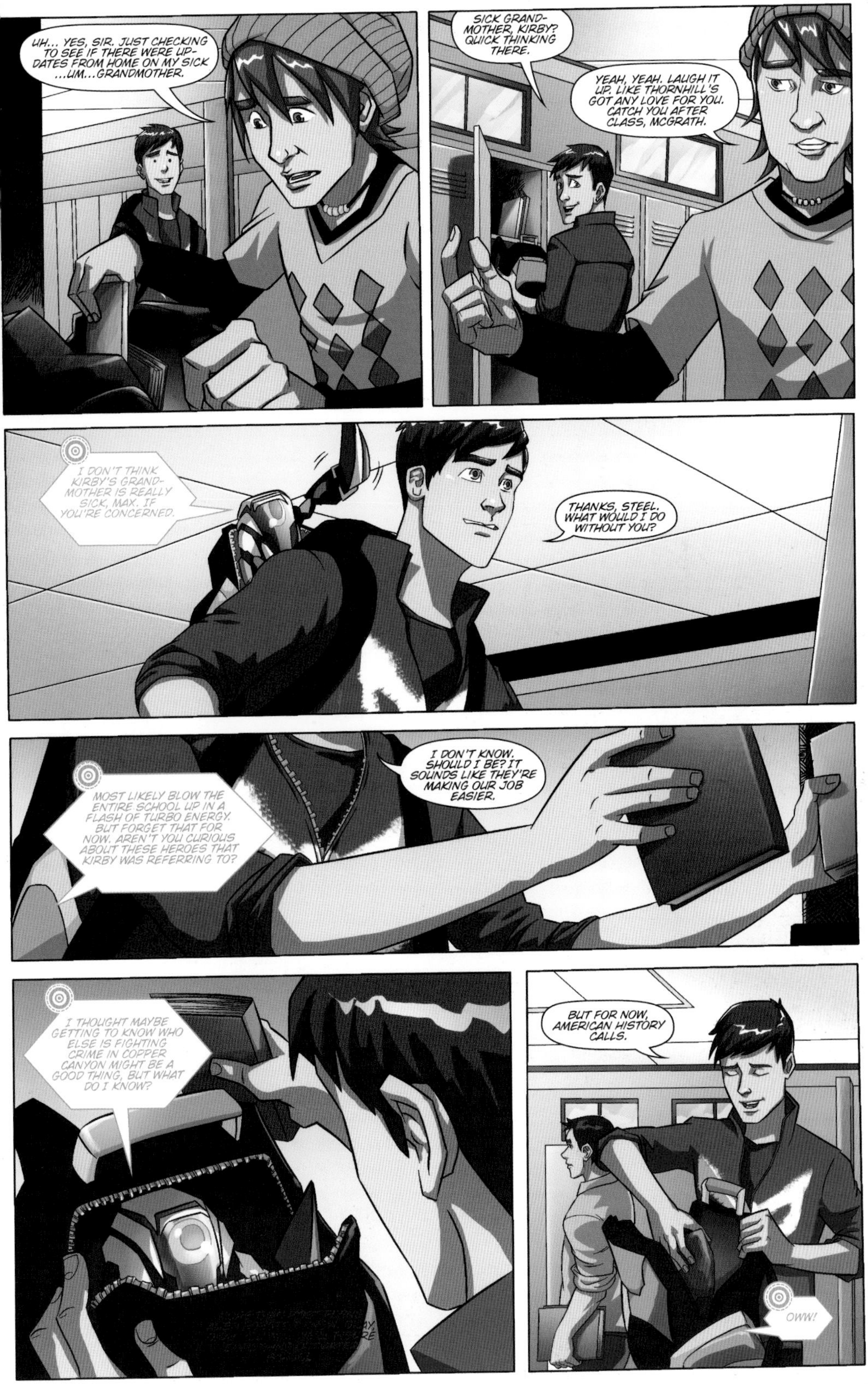
UH... YES, SIR. JUST CHECKING TO SEE IF THERE WERE UPDATES FROM HOME ON MY SICK ...UM...GRANDMOTHER.
SICK GRANDMOTHER, KIRBY? QUICK THINKING THERE.
YEAH, YEAH. LAUGH IT UP. LIKE THORNHILL'S GOT ANY LOVE FOR YOU. CATCH YOU AFTER CLASS, MCGRATH.
I DON'T THINK KIRBY'S GRANDMOTHER IS REALLY SICK, MAX. IF YOU'RE CONCERNED.
THANKS, STEEL. WHAT WOULD I DO WITHOUT YOU?
MOST LIKELY BLOW THE ENTIRE SCHOOL UP IN A FLASH OF TURBO ENERGY. BUT FORGET THAT FOR NOW. AREN'T YOU CURIOUS ABOUT THESE HEROES THAT KIRBY WAS REFERRING TO?
I DON'T KNOW. SHOULD I BE? IT SOUNDS LIKE THEY'RE MAKING OUR JOB EASIER.
I THOUGHT MAYBE GETTING TO KNOW WHO ELSE IS FIGHTING CRIME IN COPPER CANYON MIGHT BE A GOOD THING, BUT WHAT DO I KNOW?
BUT FOR NOW, AMERICAN HISTORY CALLS.
OWW!

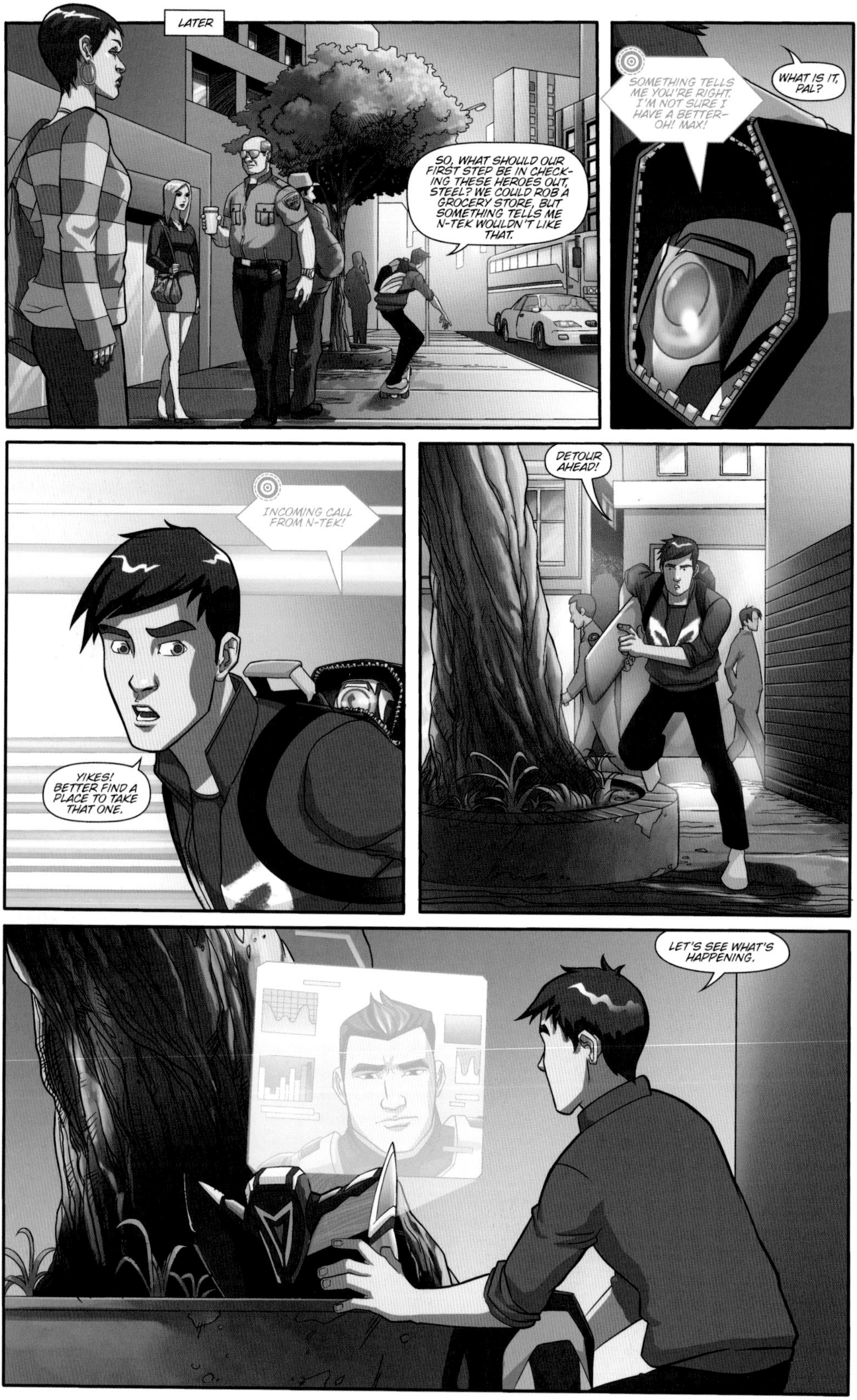
LATER
SO, WHAT SHOULD OUR FIRST STEP BE IN CHECKING THESE HEROES OUT, STEEL? WE COULD ROB A GROCERY STORE, BUT SOMETHING TELLS ME N-TEK WOULDN'T LIKE THAT.
SOMETHING TELLS ME YOU'RE RIGHT. I'M NOT SURE I HAVE A BETTER— OH! MAX!
WHAT IS IT, PAL?
INCOMING CALL FROM N-TEK!
YIKES! BETTER FIND A PLACE TO TAKE THAT ONE.
DETOUR AHEAD!
LET'S SEE WHAT'S HAPPENING.

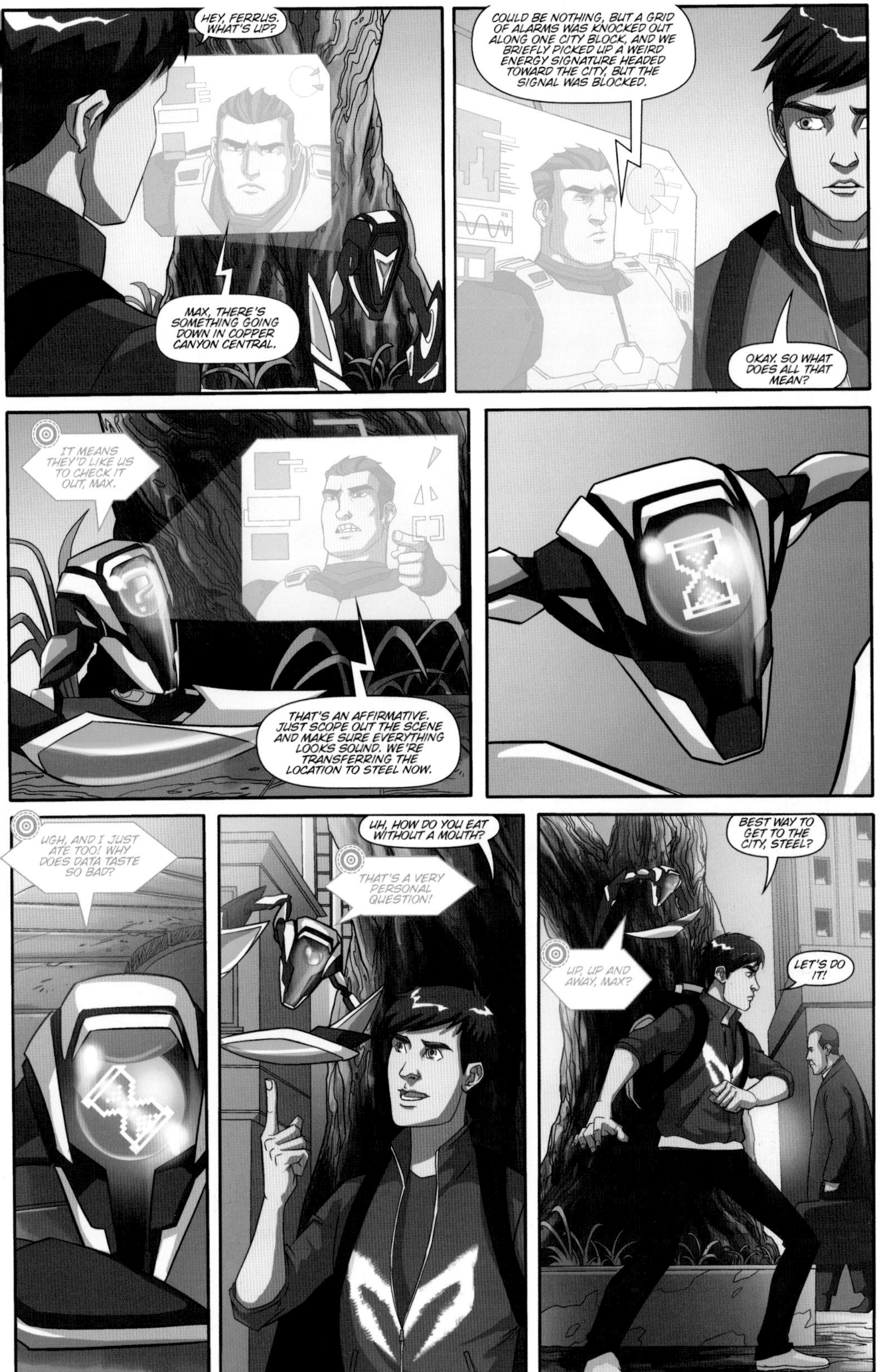
HEY, FERRUS. WHAT'S UP?
MAX, THERE'S SOMETHING GOING DOWN IN COPPER CANYON CENTRAL.
COULD BE NOTHING, BUT A GRID OF ALARMS WAS KNOCKED OUT ALONG ONE CITY BLOCK, AND WE BRIEFLY PICKED UP A WEIRD ENERGY SIGNATURE HEADED TOWARD THE CITY, BUT THE SIGNAL WAS BLOCKED.
OKAY. SO WHAT DOES ALL THAT MEAN?
IT MEANS THEY'D LIKE US TO CHECK IT OUT, MAX.
THAT'S AN AFFIRMATIVE. JUST SCOPE OUT THE SCENE AND MAKE SURE EVERYTHING LOOKS SOUND. WE'RE TRANSFERRING THE LOCATION TO STEEL NOW.
UGH, AND I JUST ATE TOO! WHY DOES DATA TASTE SO BAD?
UH, HOW DO YOU EAT WITHOUT A MOUTH?
THAT'S A VERY PERSONAL QUESTION!
BEST WAY TO GET TO THE CITY, STEEL?
UP, UP AND AWAY, MAX?
LET'S DO IT!

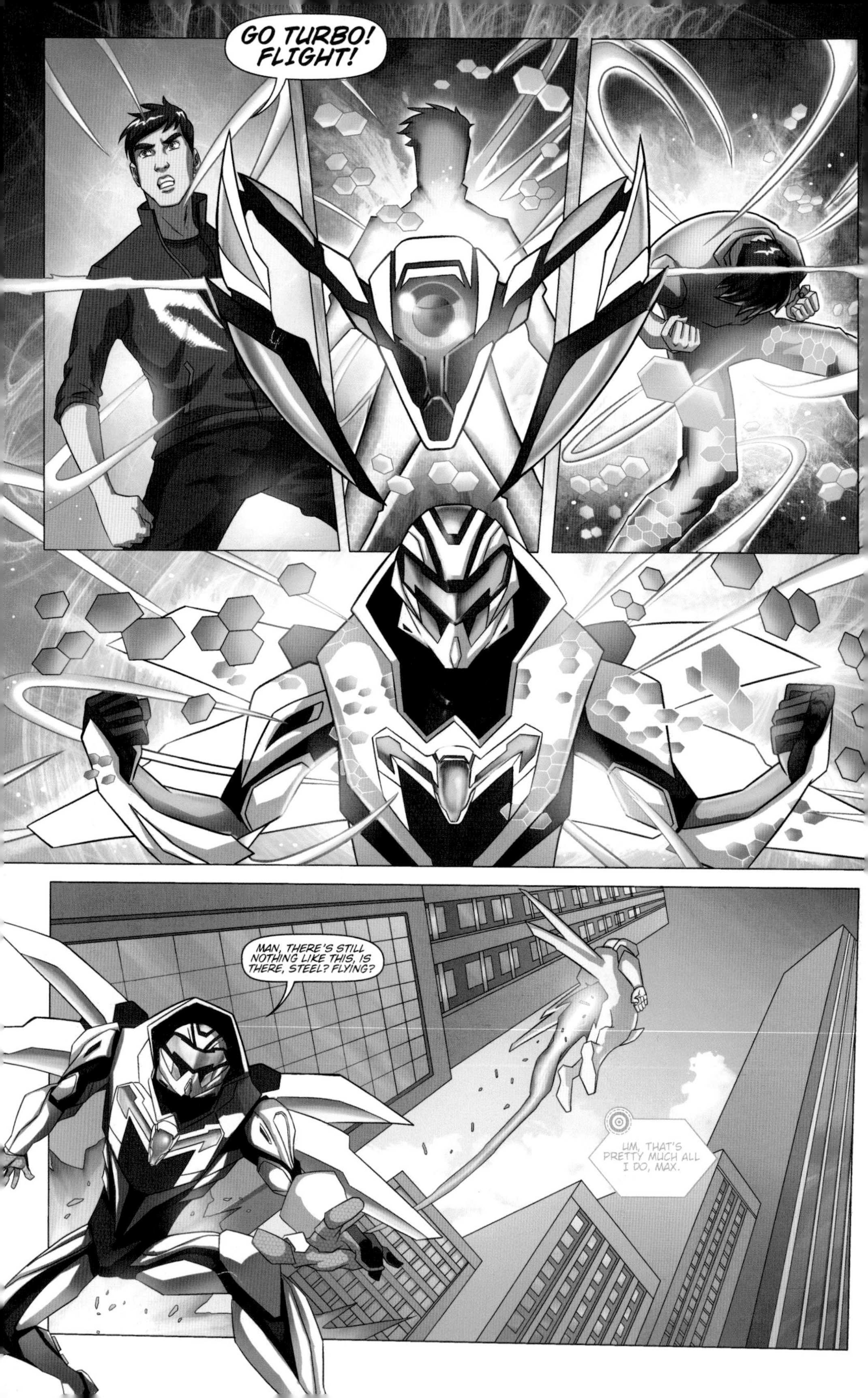
GO TURBO! FLIGHT!
MAN, THERE'S STILL NOTHING LIKE THIS, IS THERE, STEEL? FLYING?
UM, THAT'S PRETTY MUCH ALL I DO, MAX.

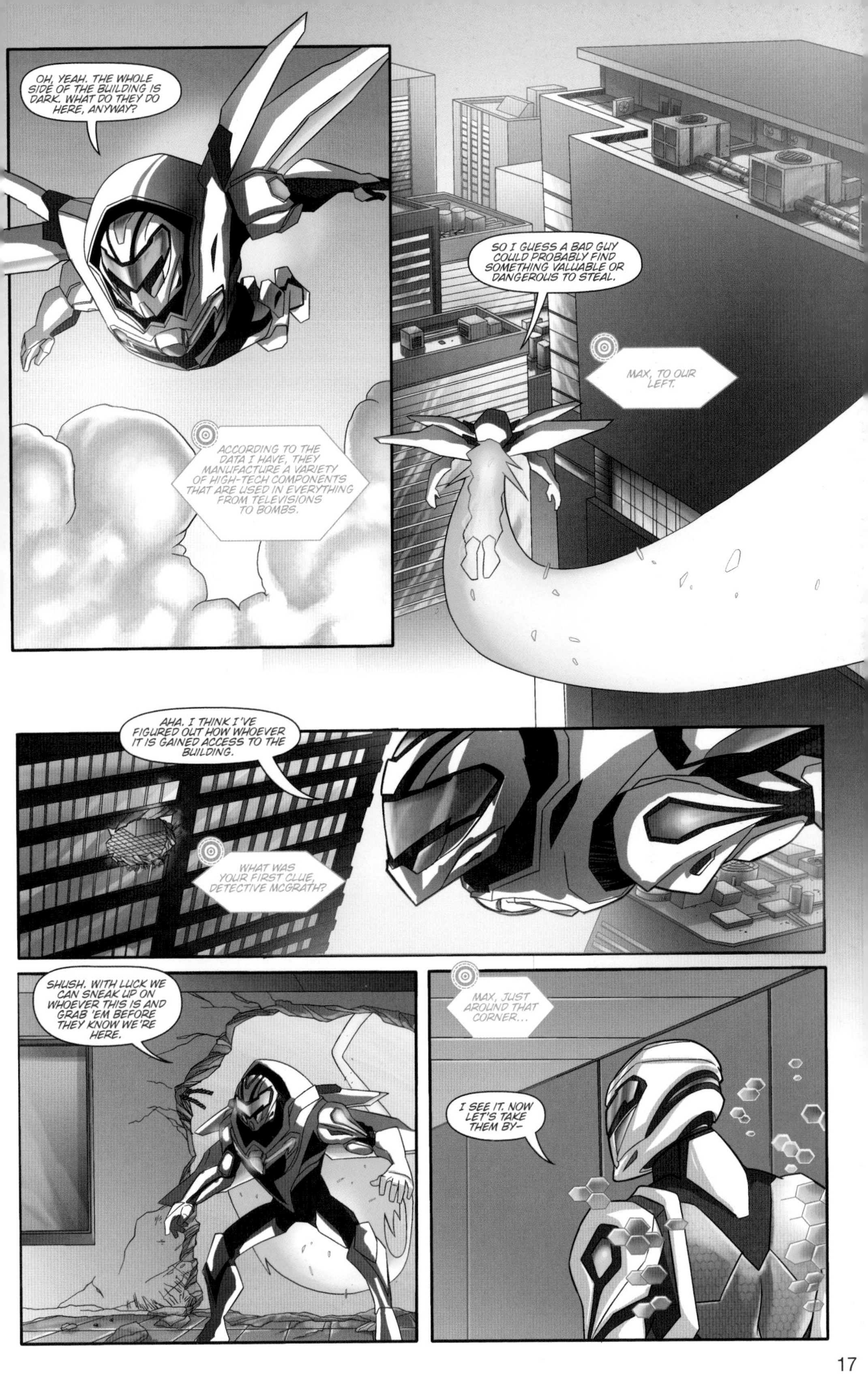

OH, YEAH. THE WHOLE SIDE OF THE BUILDING IS DARK. WHAT DO THEY DO HERE, ANYWAY?
ACCORDING TO THE DATA I HAVE, THEY MANUFACTURE A VARIETY OF HIGH-TECH COMPONENTS THAT ARE USED IN EVERYTHING FROM TELEVISIONS TO BOMBS.
SO I GUESS A BAD GUY COULD PROBABLY FIND SOMETHING VALUABLE OR DANGEROUS TO STEAL.
MAX, TO OUR LEFT.
AHA. I THINK I'VE FIGURED OUT HOW WHOEVER IT IS GAINED ACCESS TO THE BUILDING.
WHAT WAS YOUR FIRST CLUE, DETECTIVE MCGRATH?
SHUSH. WITH LUCK WE CAN SNEAK UP ON WHOEVER THIS IS AND GRAB 'EM BEFORE THEY KNOW WE'RE HERE.
MAX, JUST AROUND THAT CORNER...
I SEE IT. NOW LET'S TAKE THEM BY-

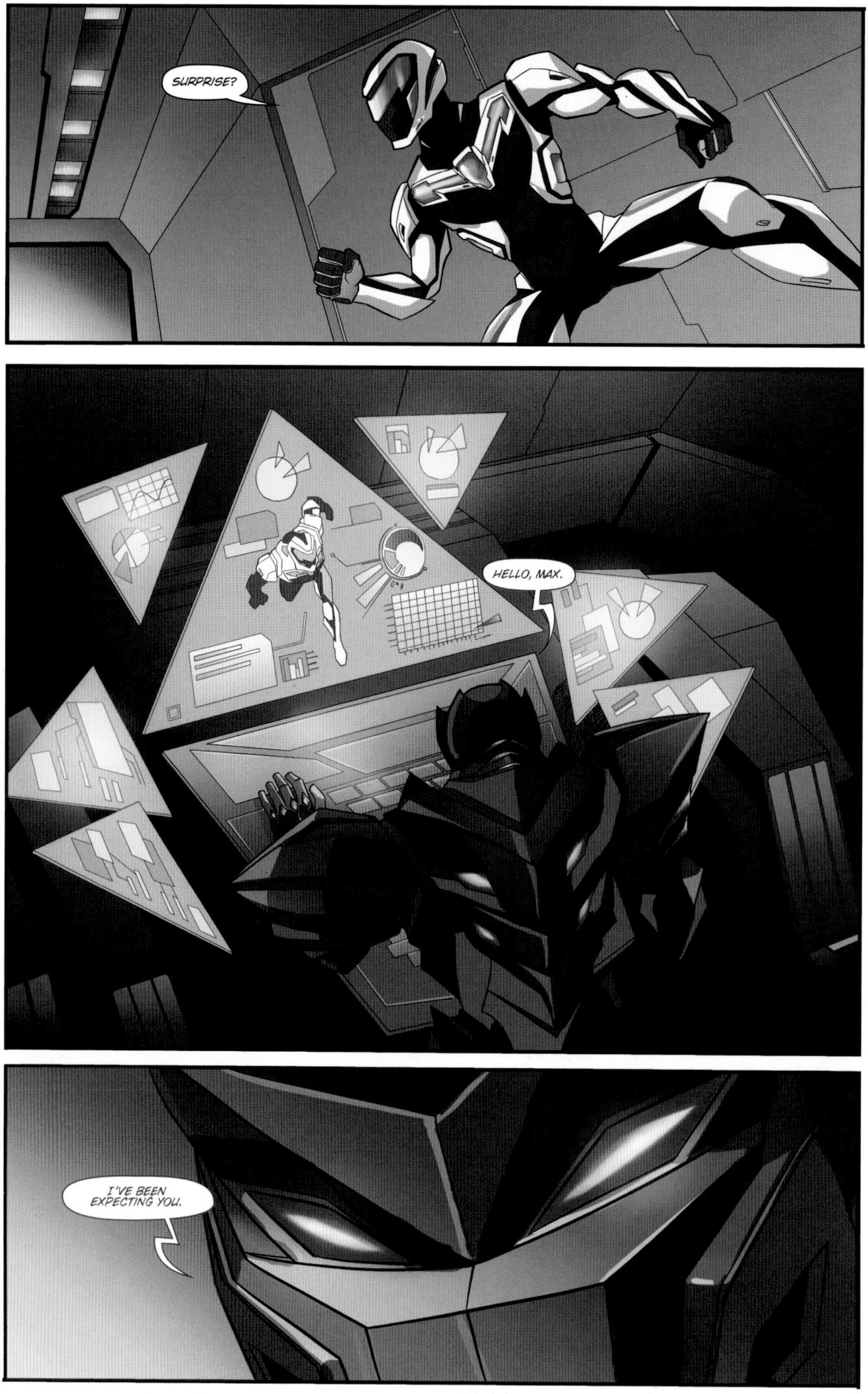
SURPRISE?
HELLO, MAX.
I'VE BEEN EXPECTING YOU.

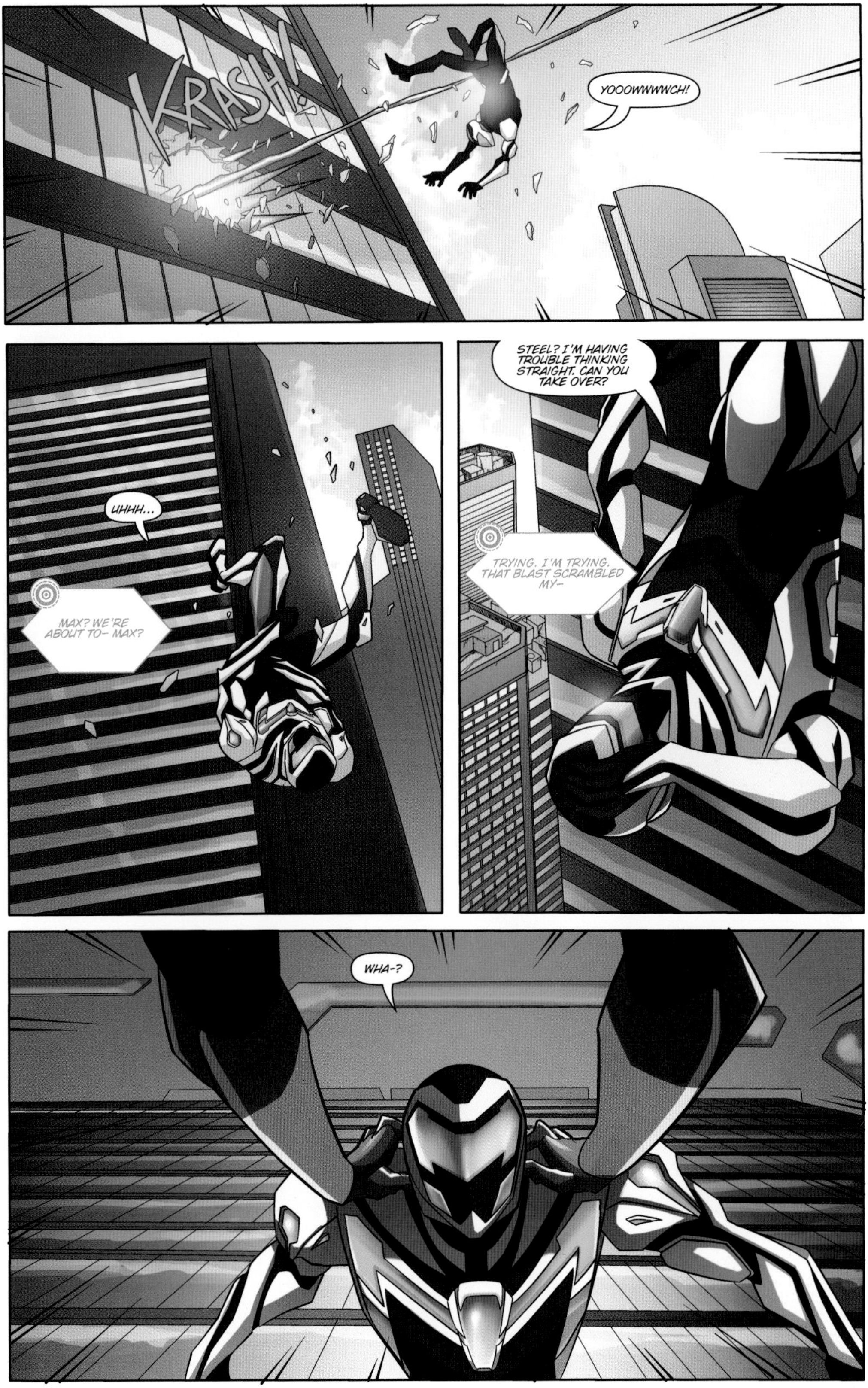
KRASH!
YOOOWWWWCH!
UHHH...
MAX? WE'RE ABOUT TO- MAX?
STEEL? I'M HAVING TROUBLE THINKING STRAIGHT. CAN YOU TAKE OVER?
TRYING. I'M TRYING. THAT BLAST SCRAMBLED MY-
WHA-?

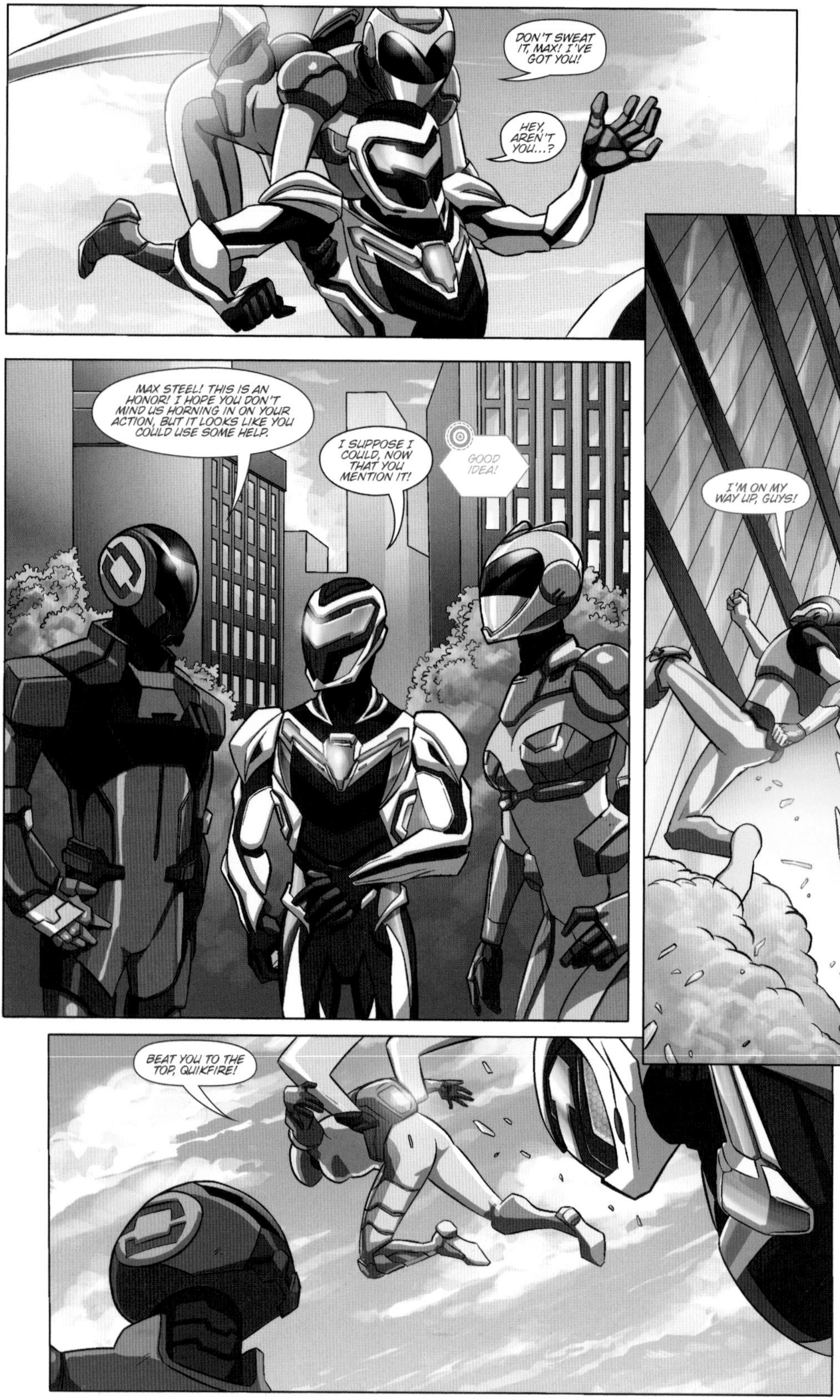
DON'T SWEAT IT, MAX! I'VE GOT YOU!
HEY, AREN'T YOU...?
MAX STEEL! THIS IS AN HONOR! I HOPE YOU DON'T MIND US HORNING IN ON YOUR ACTION, BUT IT LOOKS LIKE YOU COULD USE SOME HELP.
I SUPPOSE I COULD, NOW THAT YOU MENTION IT!
GOOD IDEA!
I'M ON MY WAY UP, GUYS!
BEAT YOU TO THE TOP, QUIKFIRE!

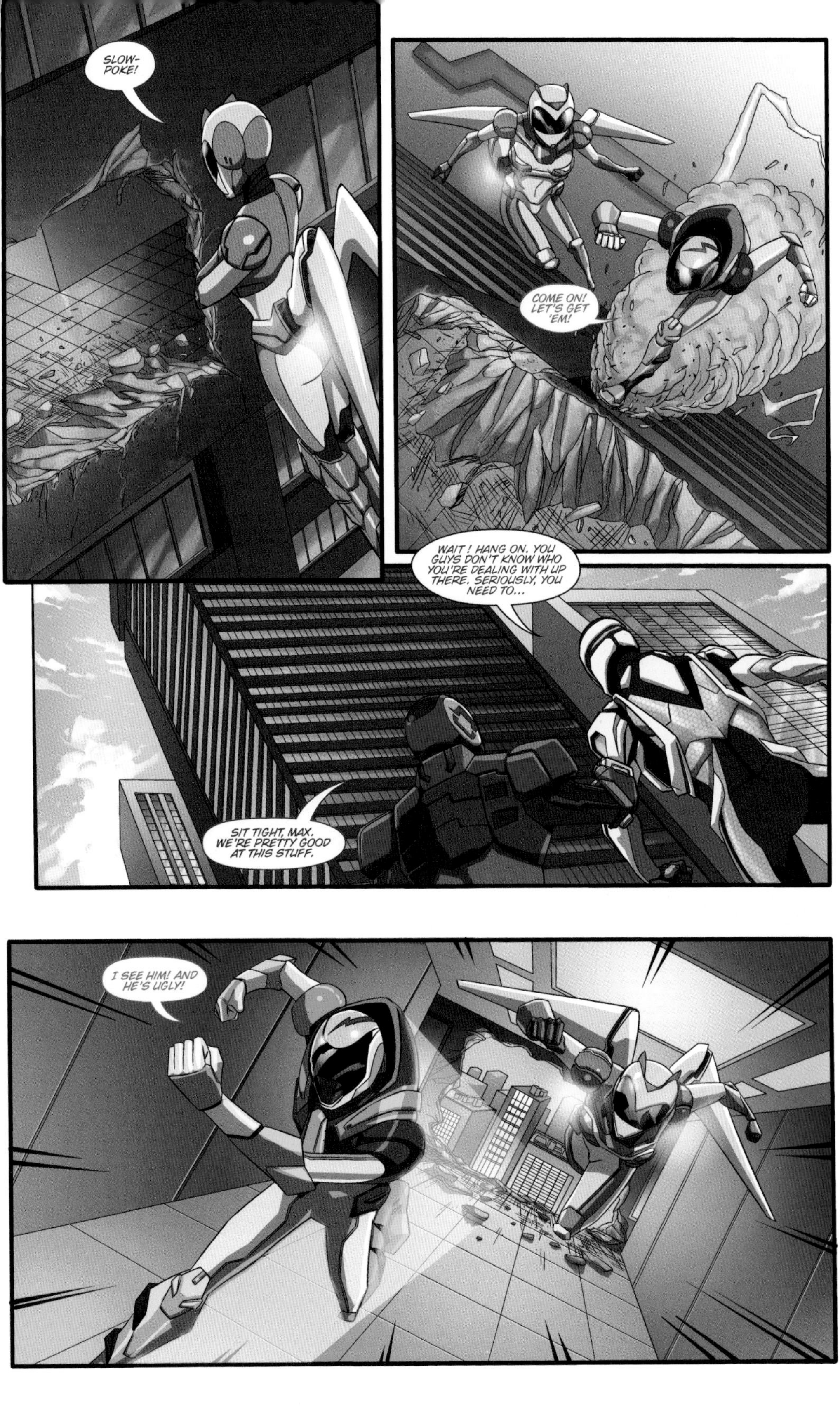
SLOW-POKE!
COME ON! LET'S GET 'EM!
WAIT ! HANG ON. YOU GUYS DON'T KNOW WHO YOU'RE DEALING WITH UP THERE. SERIOUSLY, YOU NEED TO...
SIT TIGHT, MAX. WE'RE PRETTY GOOD AT THIS STUFF.
I SEE HIM! AND HE'S UGLY!

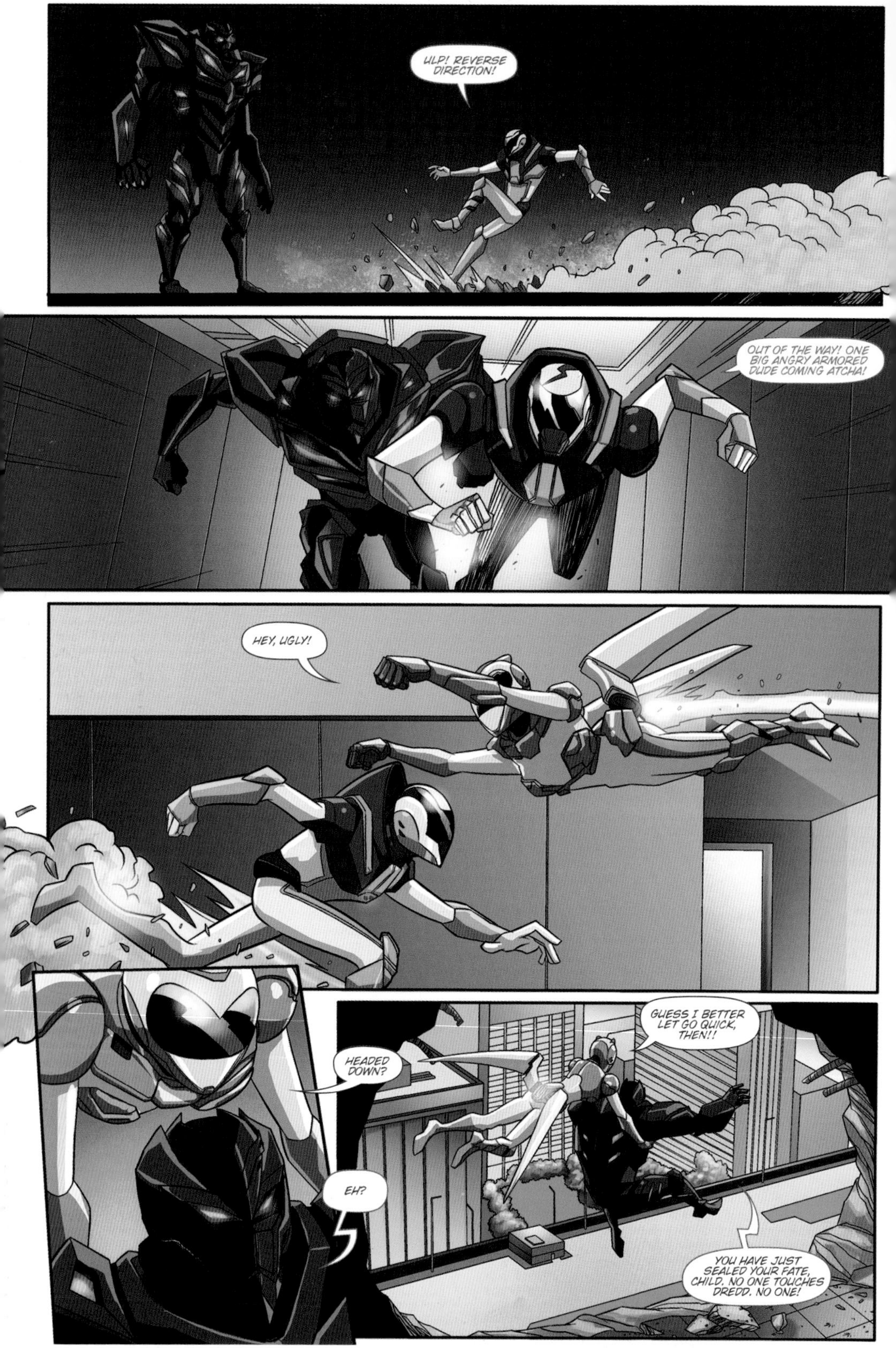

ULP! REVERSE DIRECTION!
OUT OF THE WAY! ONE BIG ANGRY ARMORED DUDE COMING ATCHA!
HEY, UGLY!
HEADED DOWN?
EH?
GUESS I BETTER LET GO QUICK, THEN!!
YOU HAVE JUST SEALED YOUR FATE, CHILD. NO ONE TOUCHES DREDD. NO ONE!

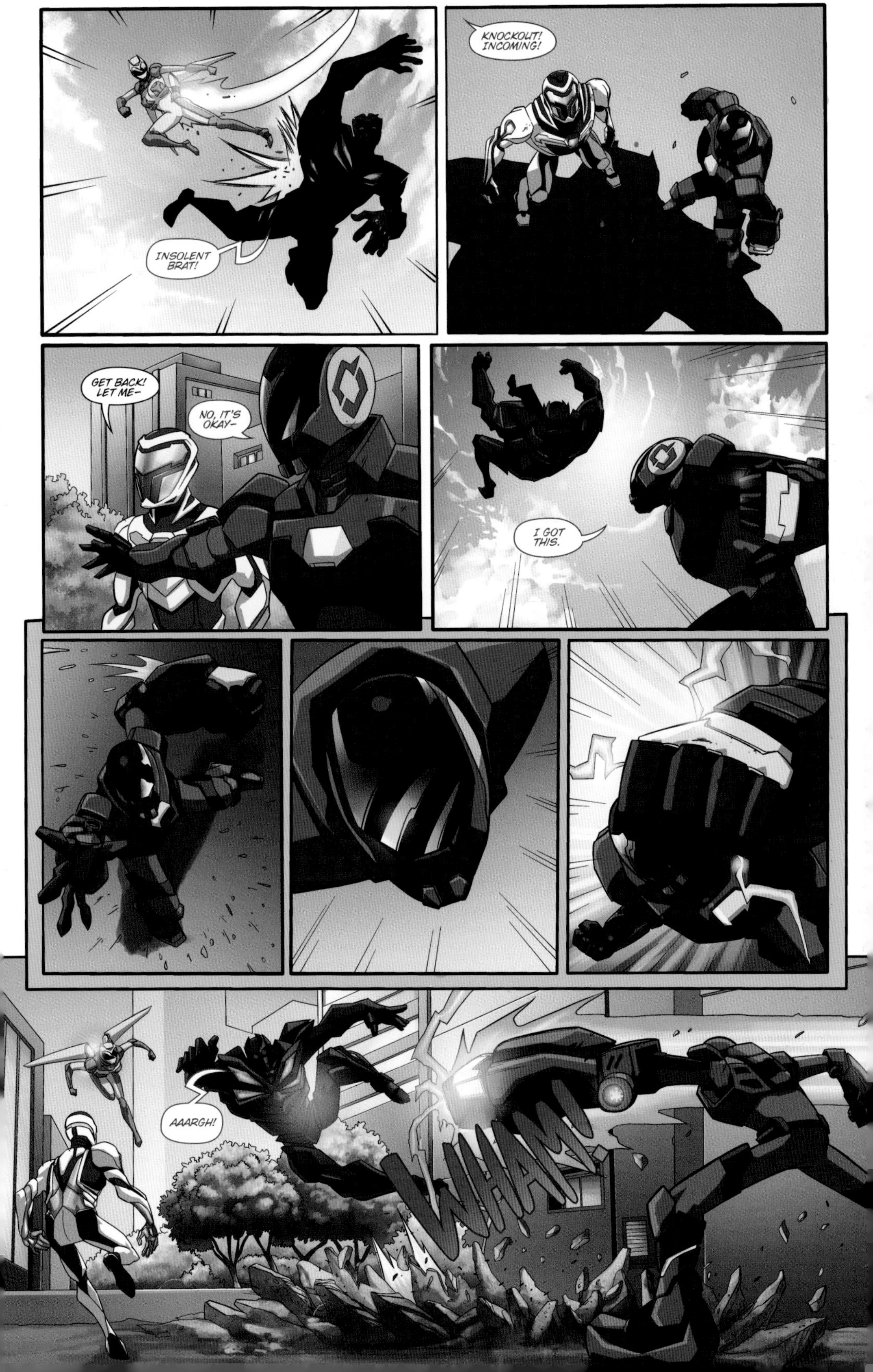
INSOLENT BRAT!
KNOCKOUT! INCOMING!
GET BACK! LET ME-
NO, IT'S OKAY-
I GOT THIS.
AAARGH!
WHAM

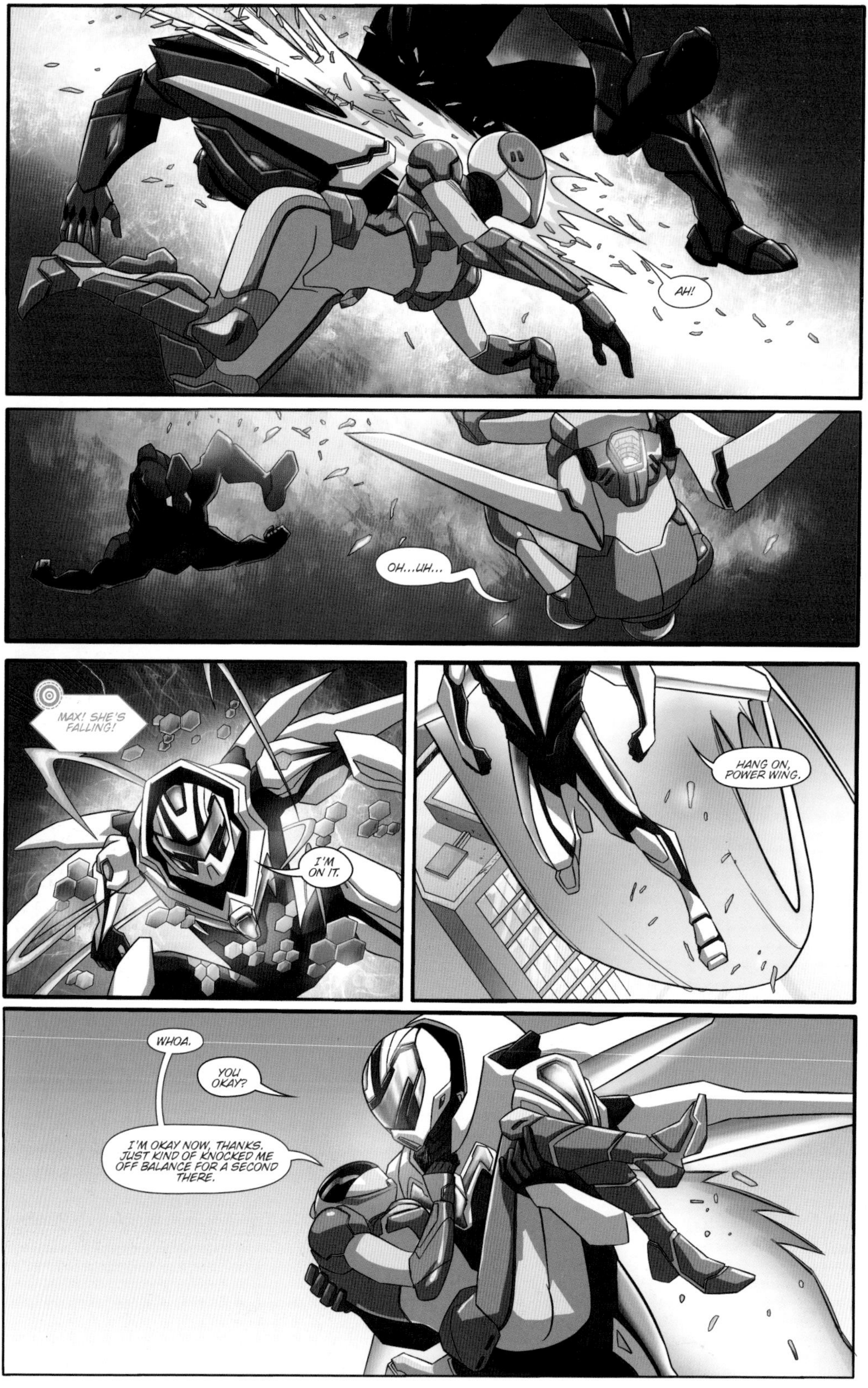
AH!
OH...UH...
MAX! SHE'S FALLING!
I'M ON IT.
HANG ON, POWER WING.
WHOA.
YOU OKAY?
I'M OKAY NOW, THANKS. JUST KIND OF KNOCKED ME OFF BALANCE FOR A SECOND THERE.

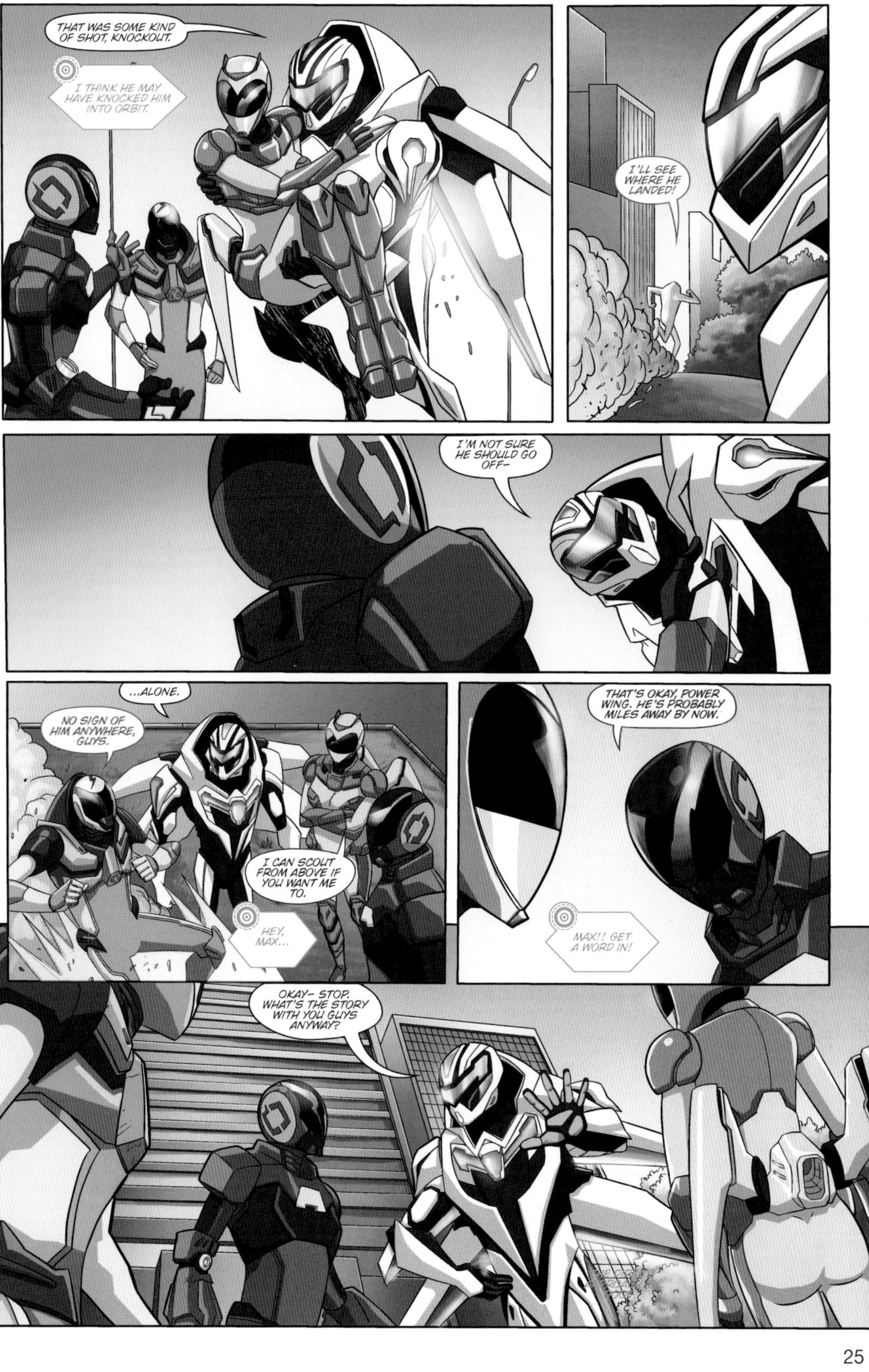
THAT WAS SOME KIND OF SHOT, KNOCKOUT.
I THINK HE MAY HAVE KNOCKED HIM INTO ORBIT.
I'LL SEE WHERE HE LANDED!
I'M NOT SURE HE SHOULD GO OFF–
...ALONE.
NO SIGN OF HIM ANYWHERE, GUYS.
I CAN SCOUT FROM ABOVE IF YOU WANT ME TO.
HEY, MAX...
THAT'S OKAY, POWER WING. HE'S PROBABLY MILES AWAY BY NOW.
MAX!! GET A WORD IN!
OKAY– STOP. WHAT'S THE STORY WITH YOU GUYS ANYWAY?

CHAPTER 2: TEAM-UP

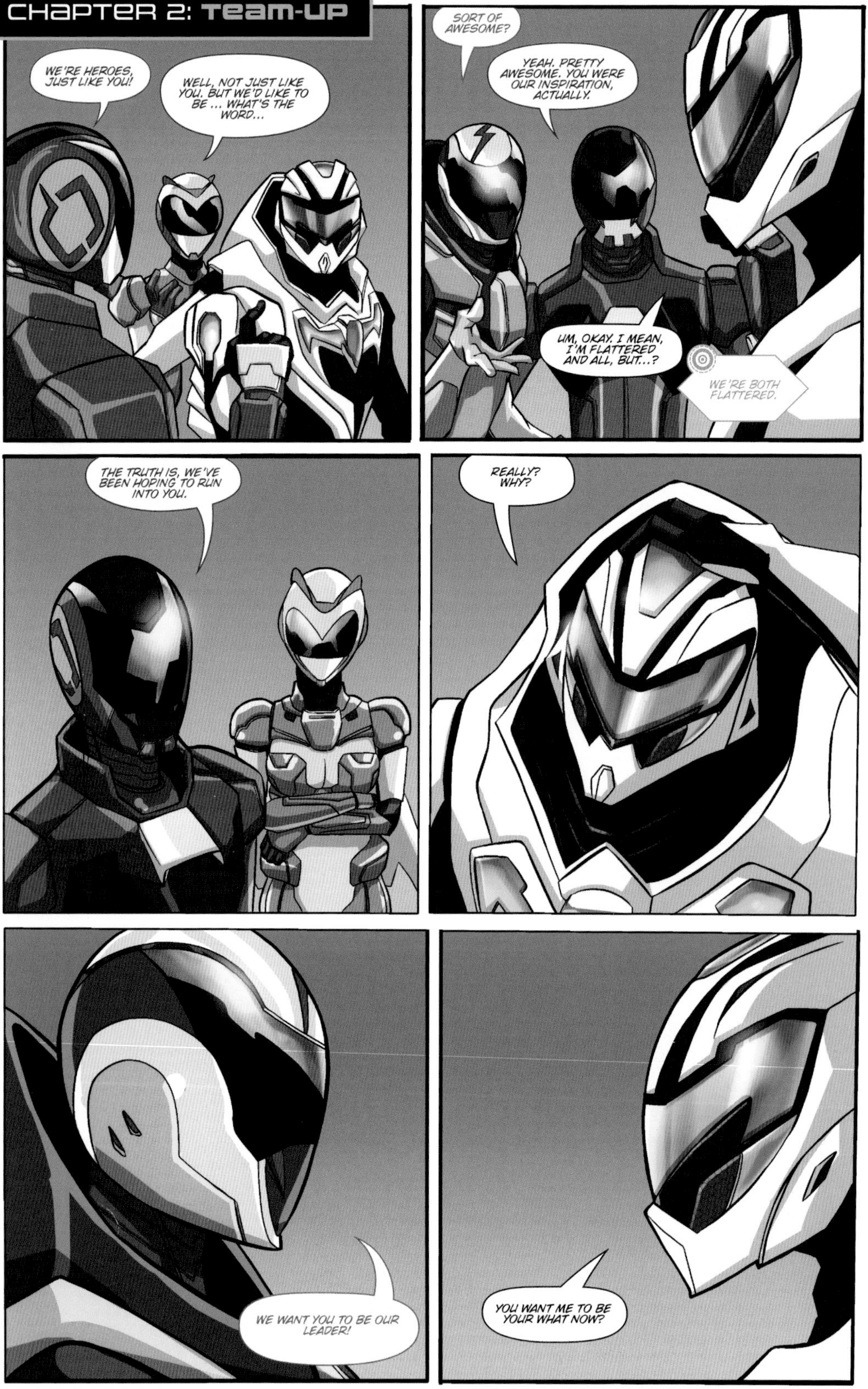
WE'RE HEROES, JUST LIKE YOU!
WELL, NOT JUST LIKE YOU. BUT WE'D LIKE TO BE ... WHAT'S THE WORD...
SORT OF AWESOME?
YEAH. PRETTY AWESOME. YOU WERE OUR INSPIRATION, ACTUALLY.
UM, OKAY. I MEAN, I'M FLATTERED AND ALL, BUT...?
WE'RE BOTH FLATTERED.
THE TRUTH IS, WE'VE BEEN HOPING TO RUN INTO YOU.
REALLY? WHY?
WE WANT YOU TO BE OUR LEADER!
YOU WANT ME TO BE YOUR WHAT NOW?

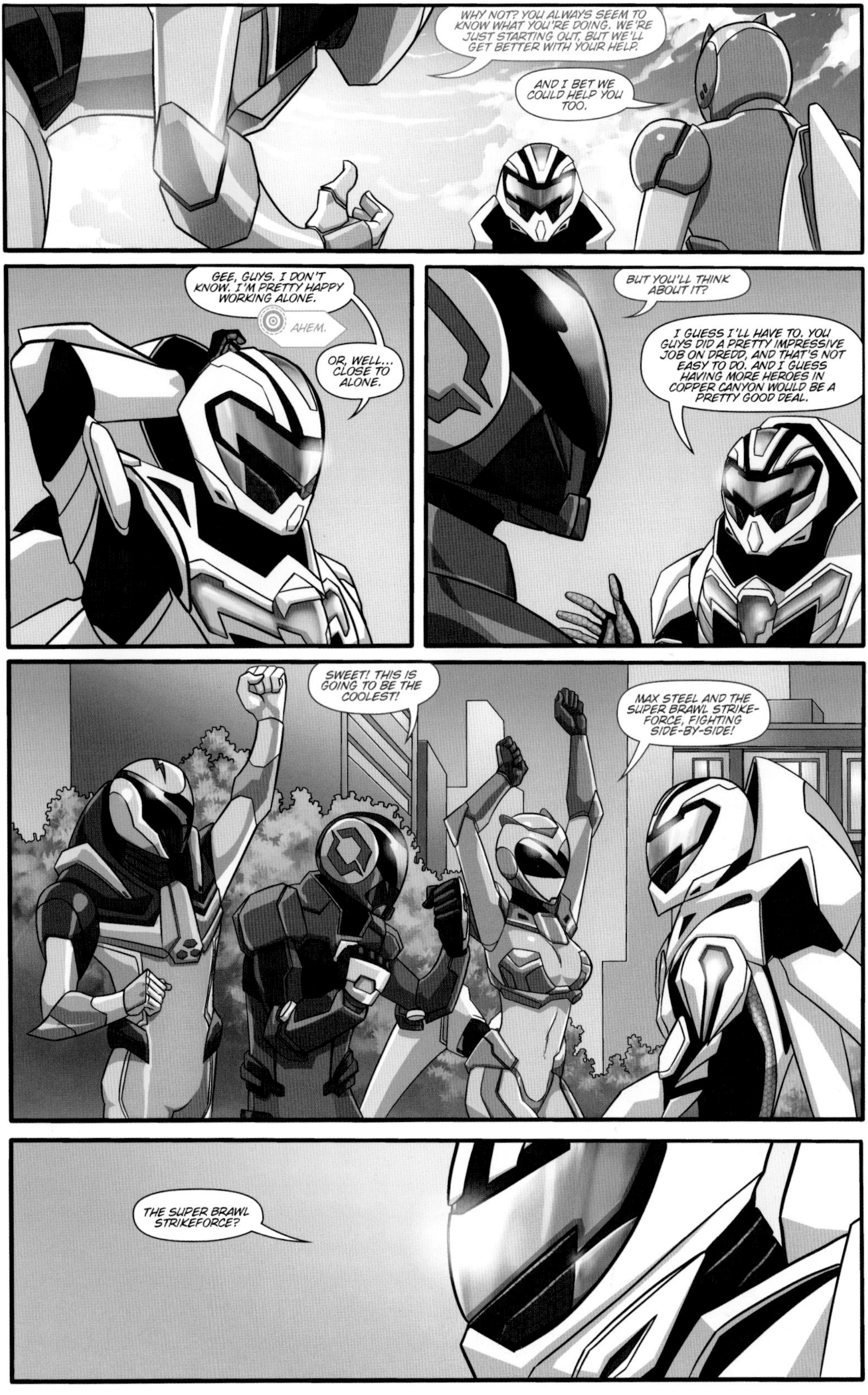
WHY NOT? YOU ALWAYS SEEM TO KNOW WHAT YOU'RE DOING. WE'RE JUST STARTING OUT, BUT WE'LL GET BETTER WITH YOUR HELP.
AND I BET WE COULD HELP YOU TOO.
GEE, GUYS. I DON'T KNOW. I'M PRETTY HAPPY WORKING ALONE.
AHEM.
OR, WELL... CLOSE TO ALONE.
BUT YOU'LL THINK ABOUT IT?
I GUESS I'LL HAVE TO. YOU GUYS DID A PRETTY IMPRESSIVE JOB ON DREDD, AND THAT'S NOT EASY TO DO. AND I GUESS HAVING MORE HEROES IN COPPER CANYON WOULD BE A PRETTY GOOD DEAL.
SWEET! THIS IS GOING TO BE THE COOLEST!
MAX STEEL AND THE SUPER BRAWL STRIKE-FORCE, FIGHTING SIDE-BY-SIDE!
THE SUPER BRAWL STRIKEFORCE?

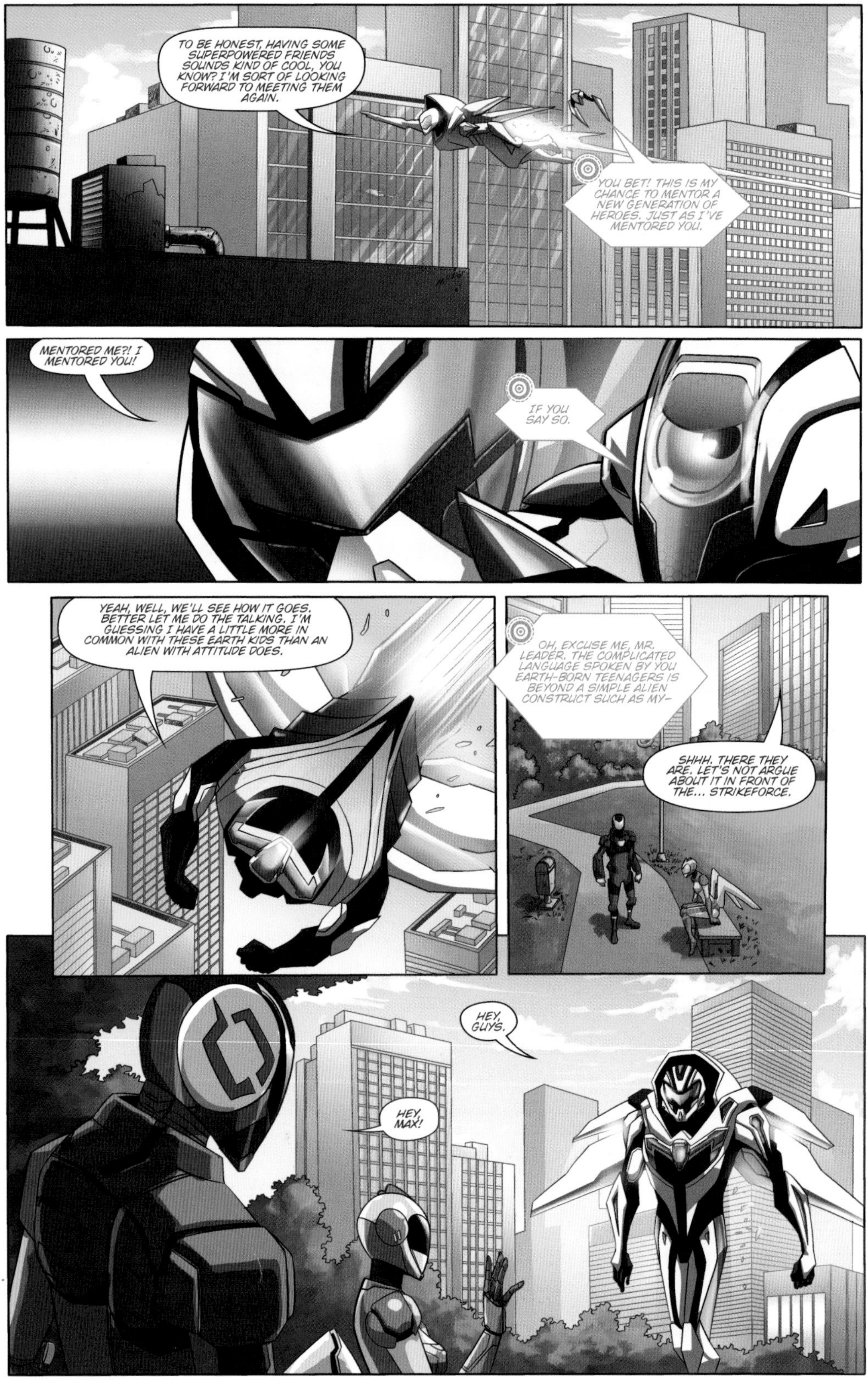
TO BE HONEST, HAVING SOME SUPERPOWERED FRIENDS SOUNDS KIND OF COOL, YOU KNOW? I'M SORT OF LOOKING FORWARD TO MEETING THEM AGAIN.
YOU BET! THIS IS MY CHANCE TO MENTOR A NEW GENERATION OF HEROES. JUST AS I'VE MENTORED YOU.
MENTORED ME?! I MENTORED YOU!
IF YOU SAY SO.
YEAH, WELL, WE'LL SEE HOW IT GOES. BETTER LET ME DO THE TALKING. I'M GUESSING I HAVE A LITTLE MORE IN COMMON WITH THESE EARTH KIDS THAN AN ALIEN WITH ATTITUDE DOES.
OH, EXCUSE ME, MR. LEADER. THE COMPLICATED LANGUAGE SPOKEN BY YOU EARTH-BORN TEENAGERS IS BEYOND A SIMPLE ALIEN CONSTRUCT SUCH AS MY-
SHHH. THERE THEY ARE. LET'S NOT ARGUE ABOUT IT IN FRONT OF THE... STRIKEFORCE.
HEY, GUYS.
HEY, MAX!

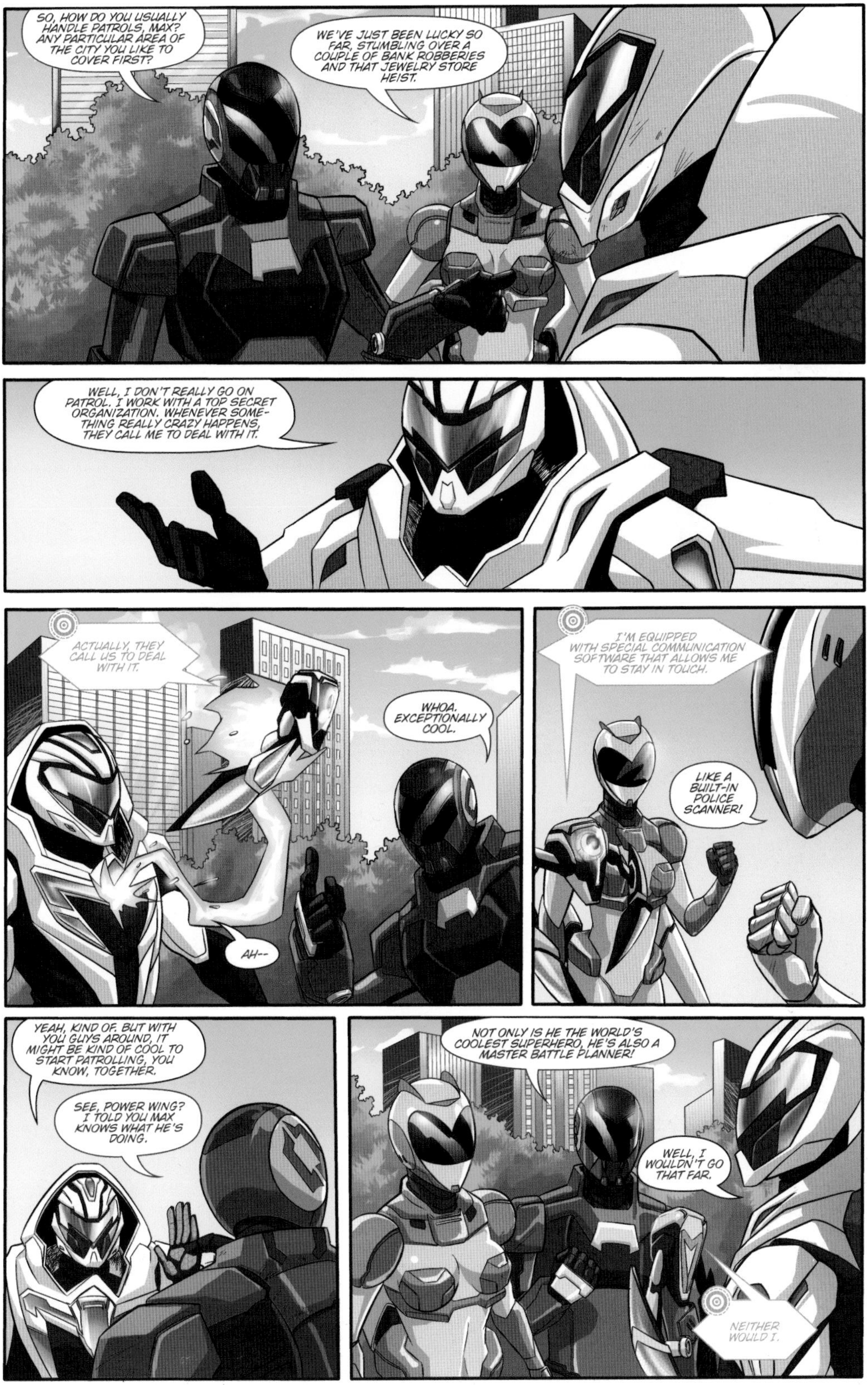
SO, HOW DO YOU USUALLY HANDLE PATROLS, MAX? ANY PARTICULAR AREA OF THE CITY YOU LIKE TO COVER FIRST?
WE'VE JUST BEEN LUCKY SO FAR, STUMBLING OVER A COUPLE OF BANK ROBBERIES AND THAT JEWELRY STORE HEIST.
WELL, I DON'T REALLY GO ON PATROL. I WORK WITH A TOP SECRET ORGANIZATION. WHENEVER SOME-THING REALLY CRAZY HAPPENS, THEY CALL ME TO DEAL WITH IT.
ACTUALLY, THEY CALL US TO DEAL WITH IT.
WHOA. EXCEPTIONALLY COOL.
AH--
I'M EQUIPPED WITH SPECIAL COMMUNICATION SOFTWARE THAT ALLOWS ME TO STAY IN TOUCH.
LIKE A BUILT-IN POLICE SCANNER!
YEAH, KIND OF. BUT WITH YOU GUYS AROUND, IT MIGHT BE KIND OF COOL TO START PATROLLING, YOU KNOW, TOGETHER.
SEE, POWER WING? I TOLD YOU MAX KNOWS WHAT HE'S DOING.
NOT ONLY IS HE THE WORLD'S COOLEST SUPERHERO, HE'S ALSO A MASTER BATTLE PLANNER!
WELL, I WOULDN'T GO THAT FAR.
NEITHER WOULD I.

HEY, HERE COMES QUIKFIRE, IN A HURRY!

I WONDERED WHERE HE WAS.

OHMYGOSHYOUGUYS-- WOULDN'TBELIEVEWHAT'S--

WHOA! WHOA! SLOW DOWN, FIRE. WE CAN'T UNDERSTAND A WORD YOU'RE SAYING.

OH, RIGHT. SORRY. I JUST GOT SO EXCITED. WE NEED TO GET BACK TO THE CANYON'S CENTRAL DISTRICT ASAP! THESE BIG, HULKING ROBOT-LOOKING DUDES ARE TEARING UP THE FINANCIAL DISTRICT!

"ROBOT-LOOKING DUDES"?

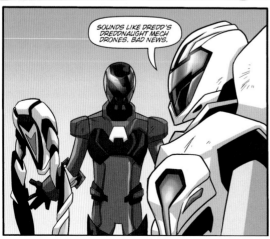

SOUNDS LIKE DREDD'S DREDDNAUGHT MECH DRONES. BAD NEWS.

MAX IS RIGHT! WE NEED TO GET DOWN THERE AS SOON AS POSSIBLE.

I'LL GO WITH YOU GUYS.

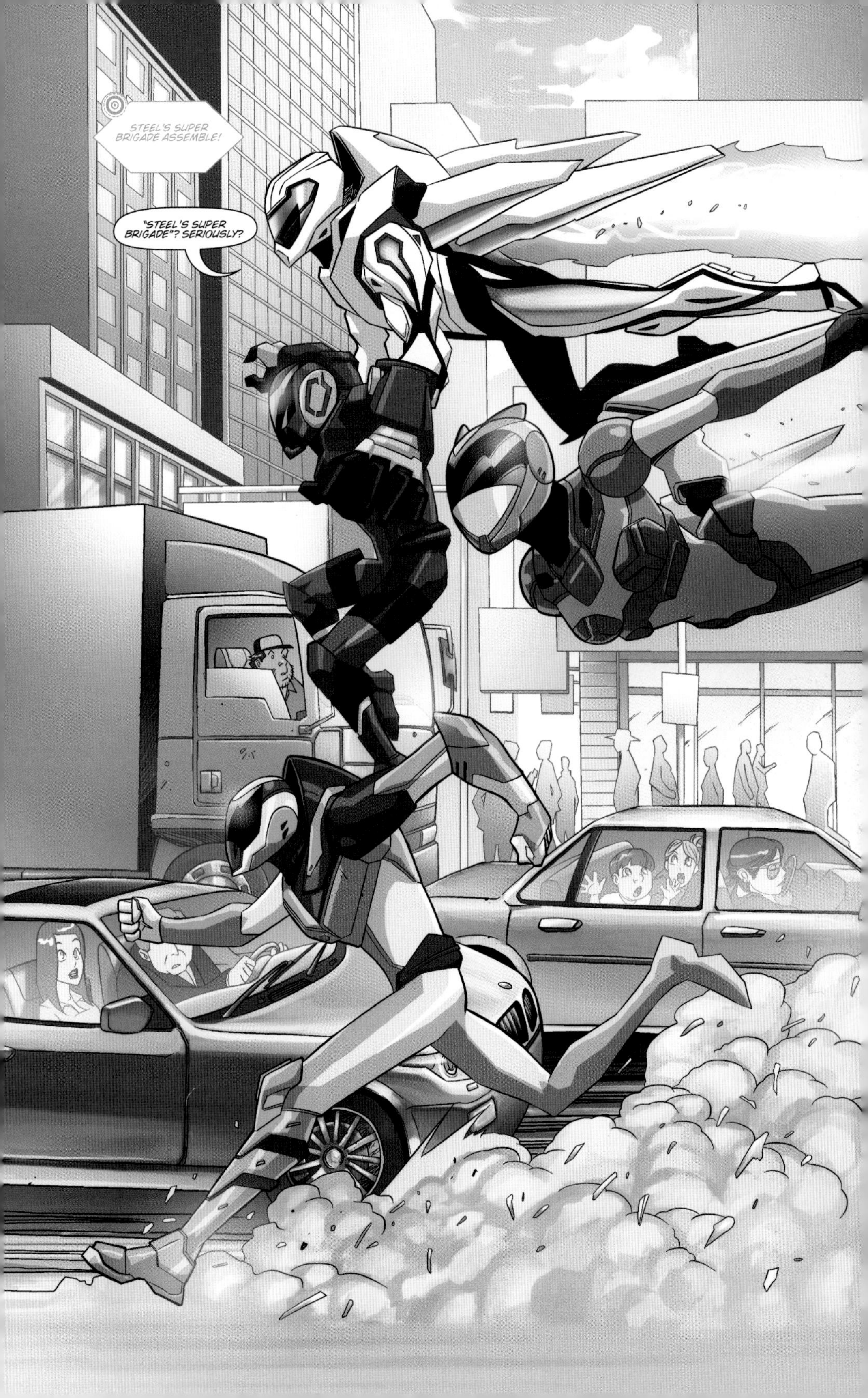
STEEL'S SUPER BRIGADE ASSEMBLE!
"STEEL'S SUPER BRIGADE"? SERIOUSLY?

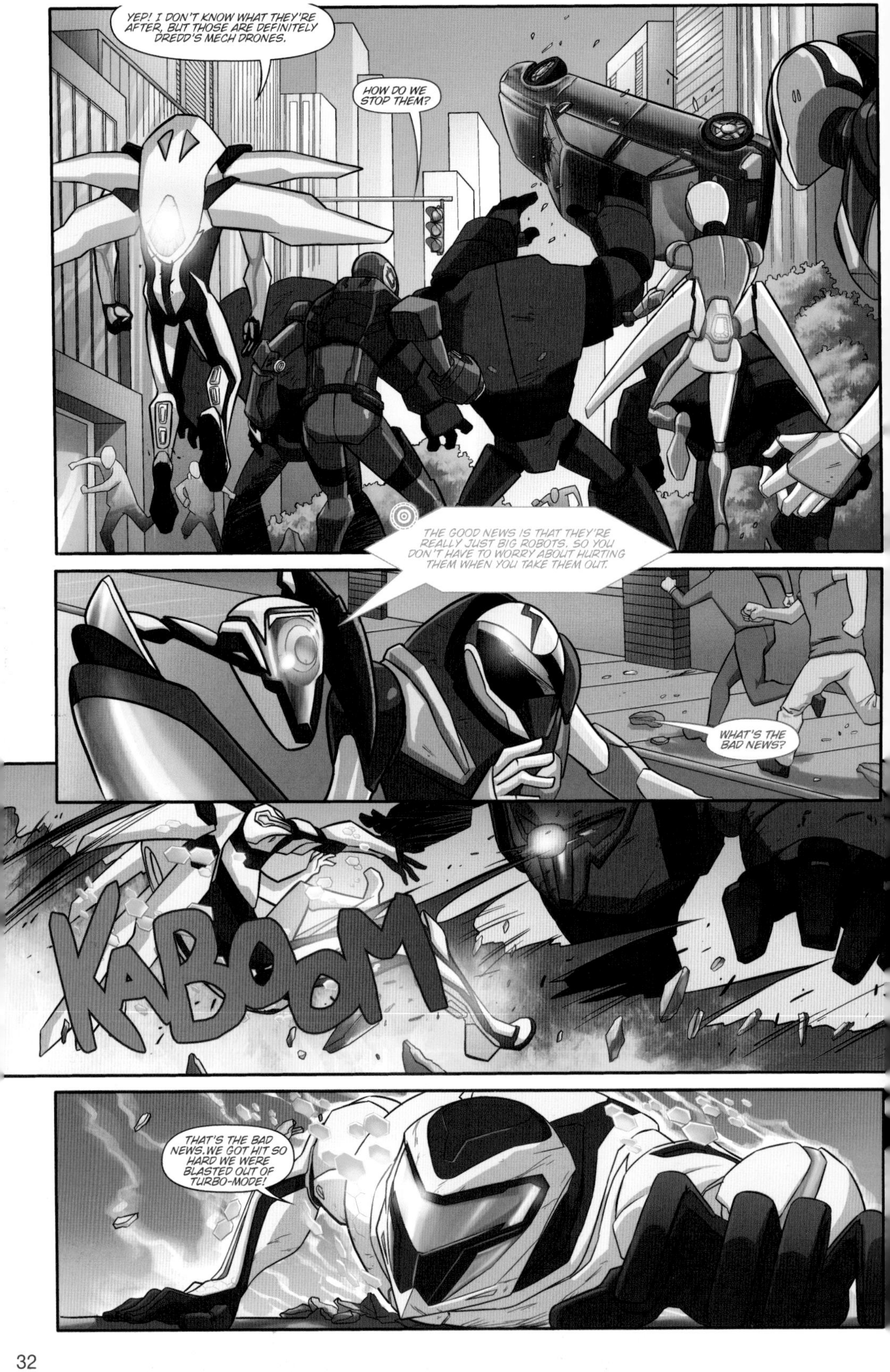

YEP! I DON'T KNOW WHAT THEY'RE AFTER, BUT THOSE ARE DEFINITELY DREDD'S MECH DRONES.
HOW DO WE STOP THEM?
THE GOOD NEWS IS THAT THEY'RE REALLY JUST BIG ROBOTS. SO YOU DON'T HAVE TO WORRY ABOUT HURTING THEM WHEN YOU TAKE THEM OUT.
WHAT'S THE BAD NEWS?
KABOOM
THAT'S THE BAD NEWS. WE GOT HIT SO HARD WE WERE BLASTED OUT OF TURBO-MODE!

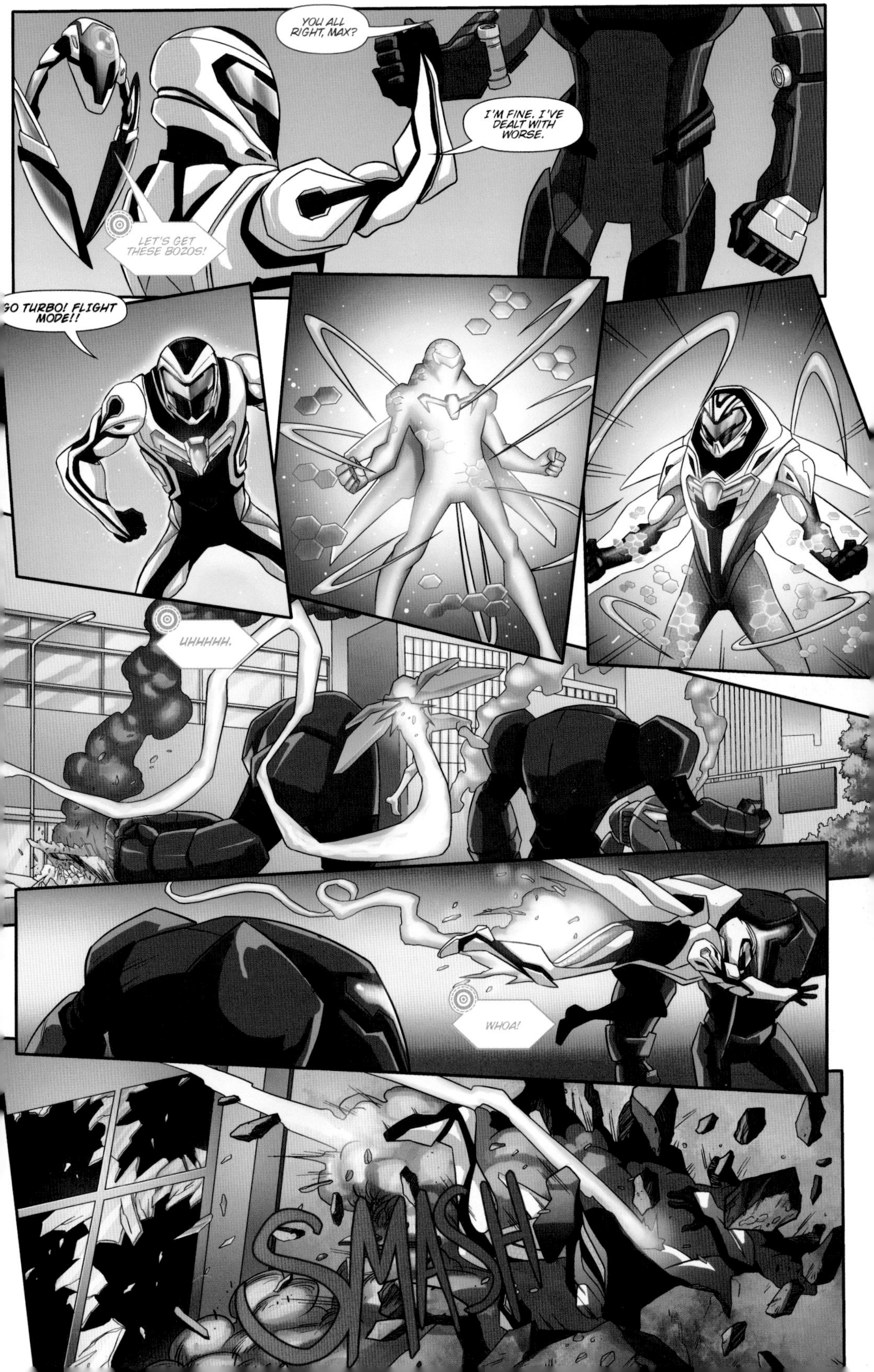
YOU ALL RIGHT, MAX?
I'M FINE. I'VE DEALT WITH WORSE.
LET'S GET THESE BOZOS!
GO TURBO! FLIGHT MODE!!
UHHHHH.
WHOA!
SMASH

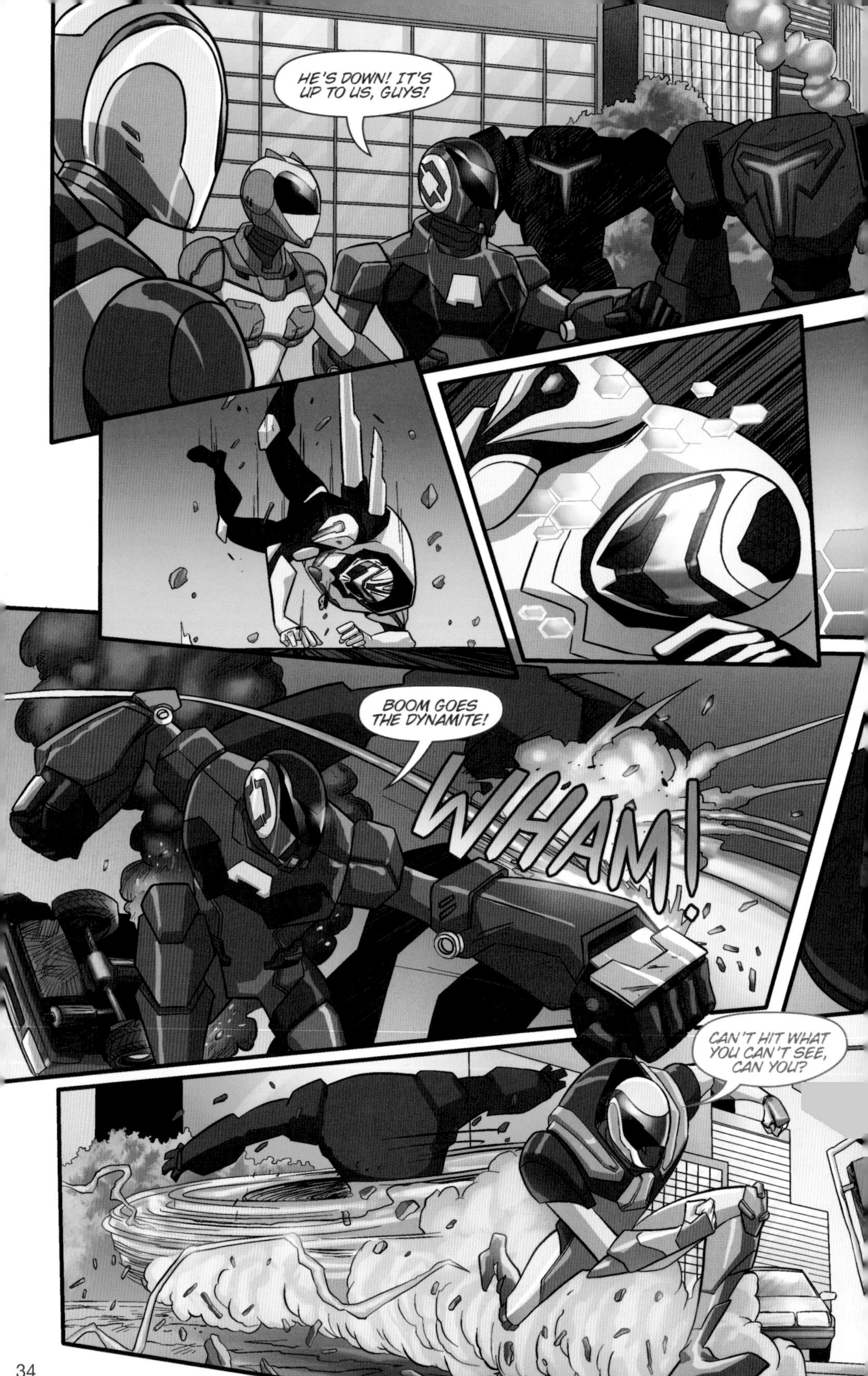

HE'S DOWN! IT'S UP TO US, GUYS!
BOOM GOES THE DYNAMITE!
WHAM!
CAN'T HIT WHAT YOU CAN'T SEE, CAN YOU?

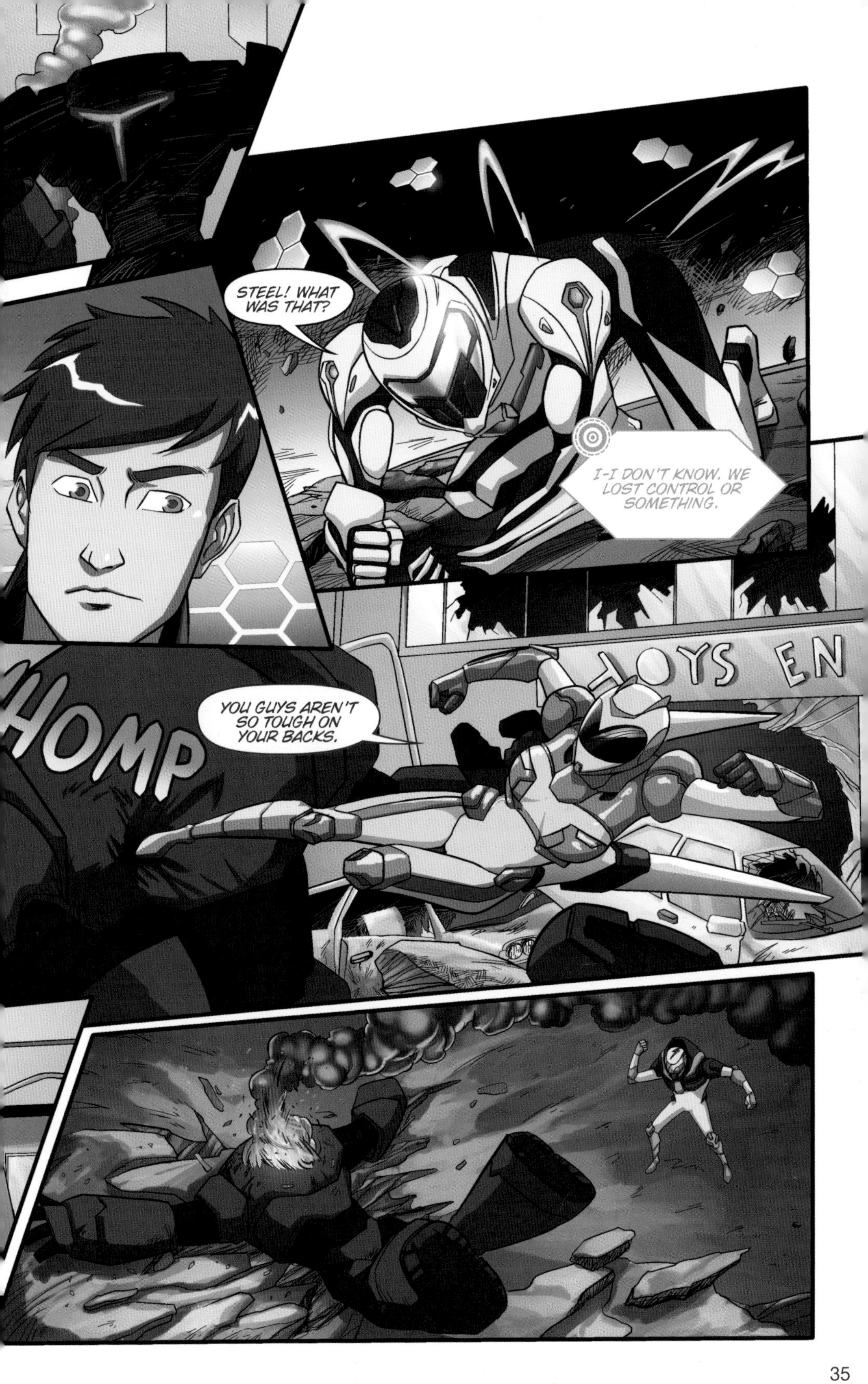
STEEL! WHAT WAS THAT?
I-I DON'T KNOW. WE LOST CONTROL OR SOMETHING.
HOMP
YOU GUYS AREN'T SO TOUGH ON YOUR BACKS.
TOYS EN

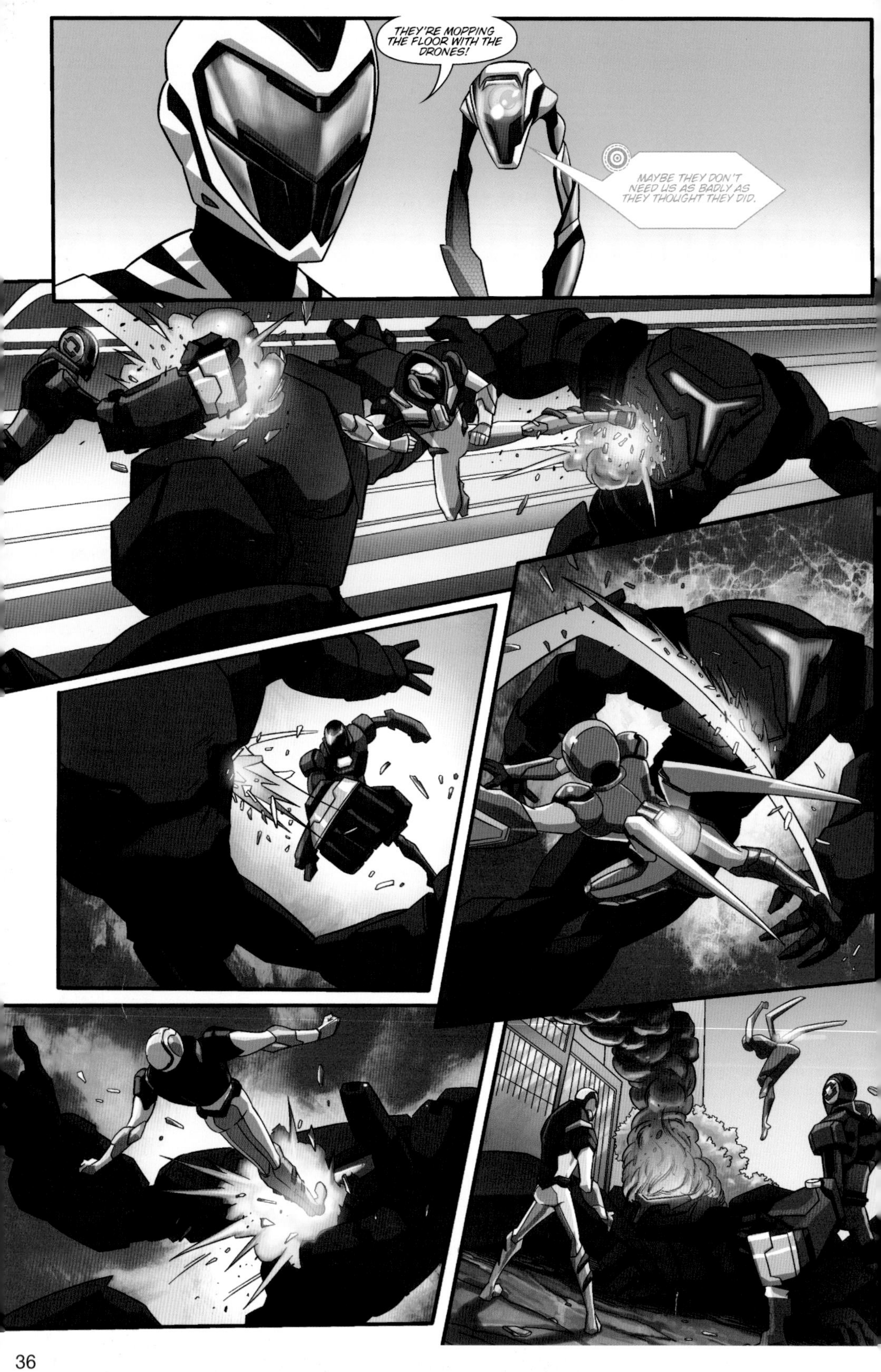
THEY'RE MOPPING THE FLOOR WITH THE DRONES!
MAYBE THEY DON'T NEED US AS BADLY AS THEY THOUGHT THEY DID.

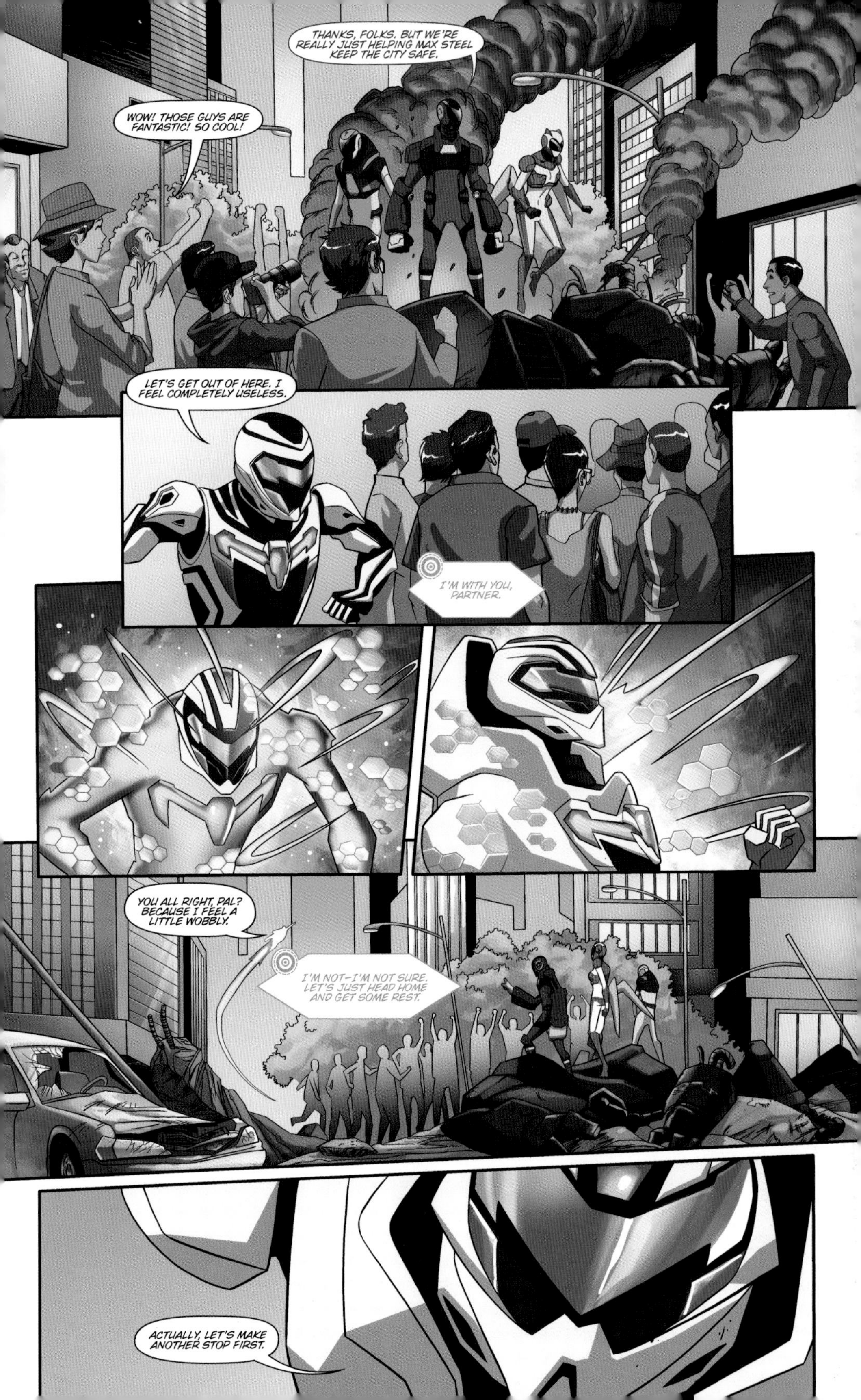
THANKS, FOLKS. BUT WE'RE REALLY JUST HELPING MAX STEEL KEEP THE CITY SAFE.
WOW! THOSE GUYS ARE FANTASTIC! SO COOL!
LET'S GET OUT OF HERE. I FEEL COMPLETELY USELESS.
I'M WITH YOU, PARTNER.
YOU ALL RIGHT, PAL? BECAUSE I FEEL A LITTLE WOBBLY.
I'M NOT—I'M NOT SURE. LET'S JUST HEAD HOME AND GET SOME REST.
ACTUALLY, LET'S MAKE ANOTHER STOP FIRST.

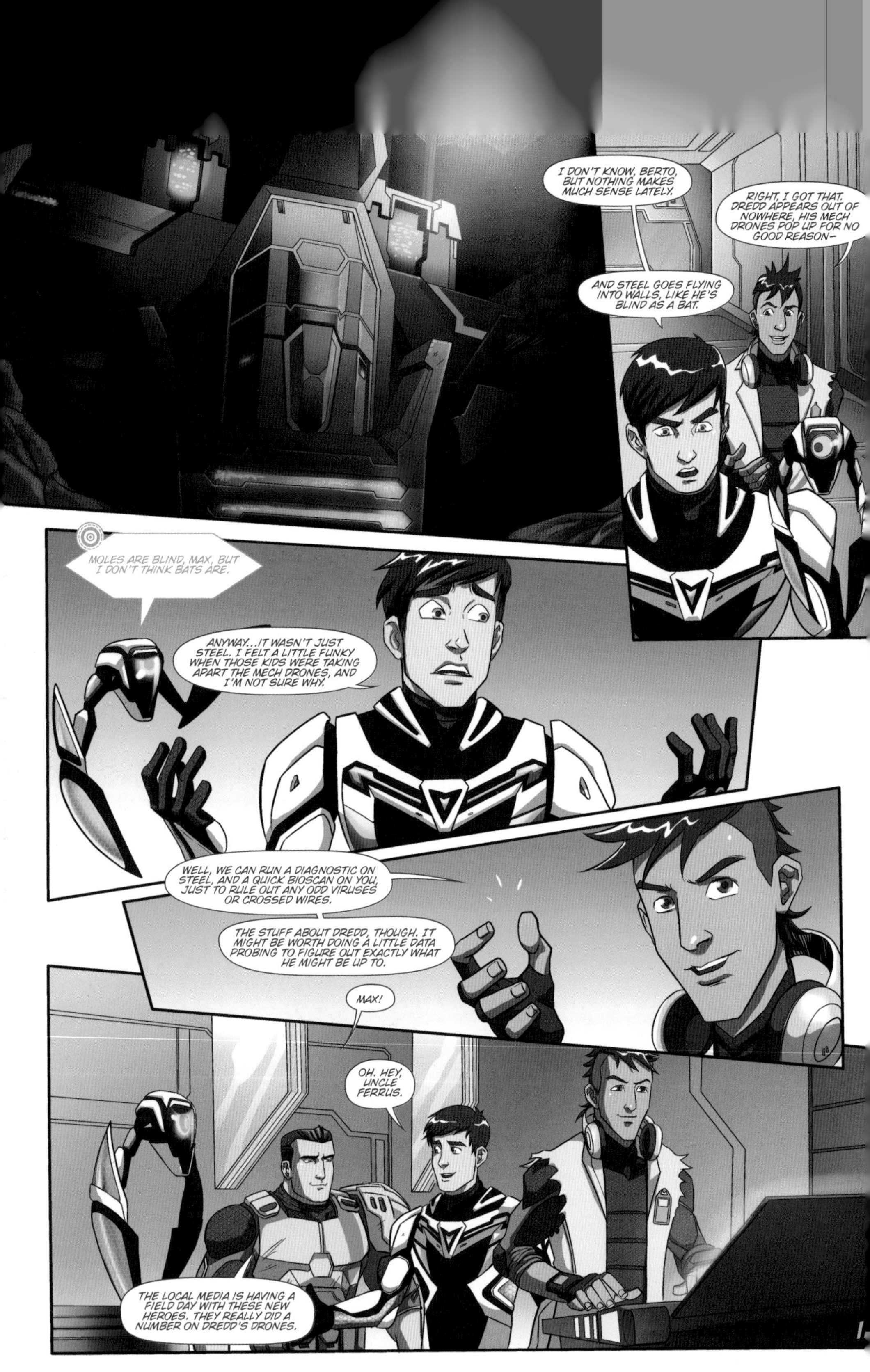
I DON'T KNOW, BERTO, BUT NOTHING MAKES MUCH SENSE LATELY.
RIGHT, I GOT THAT. DREDD APPEARS OUT OF NOWHERE, HIS MECH DRONES POP UP FOR NO GOOD REASON–
AND STEEL GOES FLYING INTO WALLS, LIKE HE'S BLIND AS A BAT.
MOLES ARE BLIND, MAX, BUT I DON'T THINK BATS ARE.
ANYWAY...IT WASN'T JUST STEEL. I FELT A LITTLE FUNKY WHEN THOSE KIDS WERE TAKING APART THE MECH DRONES, AND I'M NOT SURE WHY.
WELL, WE CAN RUN A DIAGNOSTIC ON STEEL, AND A QUICK BIOSCAN ON YOU, JUST TO RULE OUT ANY ODD VIRUSES OR CROSSED WIRES.
THE STUFF ABOUT DREDD, THOUGH. IT MIGHT BE WORTH DOING A LITTLE DATA PROBING TO FIGURE OUT EXACTLY WHAT HE MIGHT BE UP TO.
MAX!
OH. HEY, UNCLE FERRUS.
THE LOCAL MEDIA IS HAVING A FIELD DAY WITH THESE NEW HEROES. THEY REALLY DID A NUMBER ON DREDD'S DRONES.

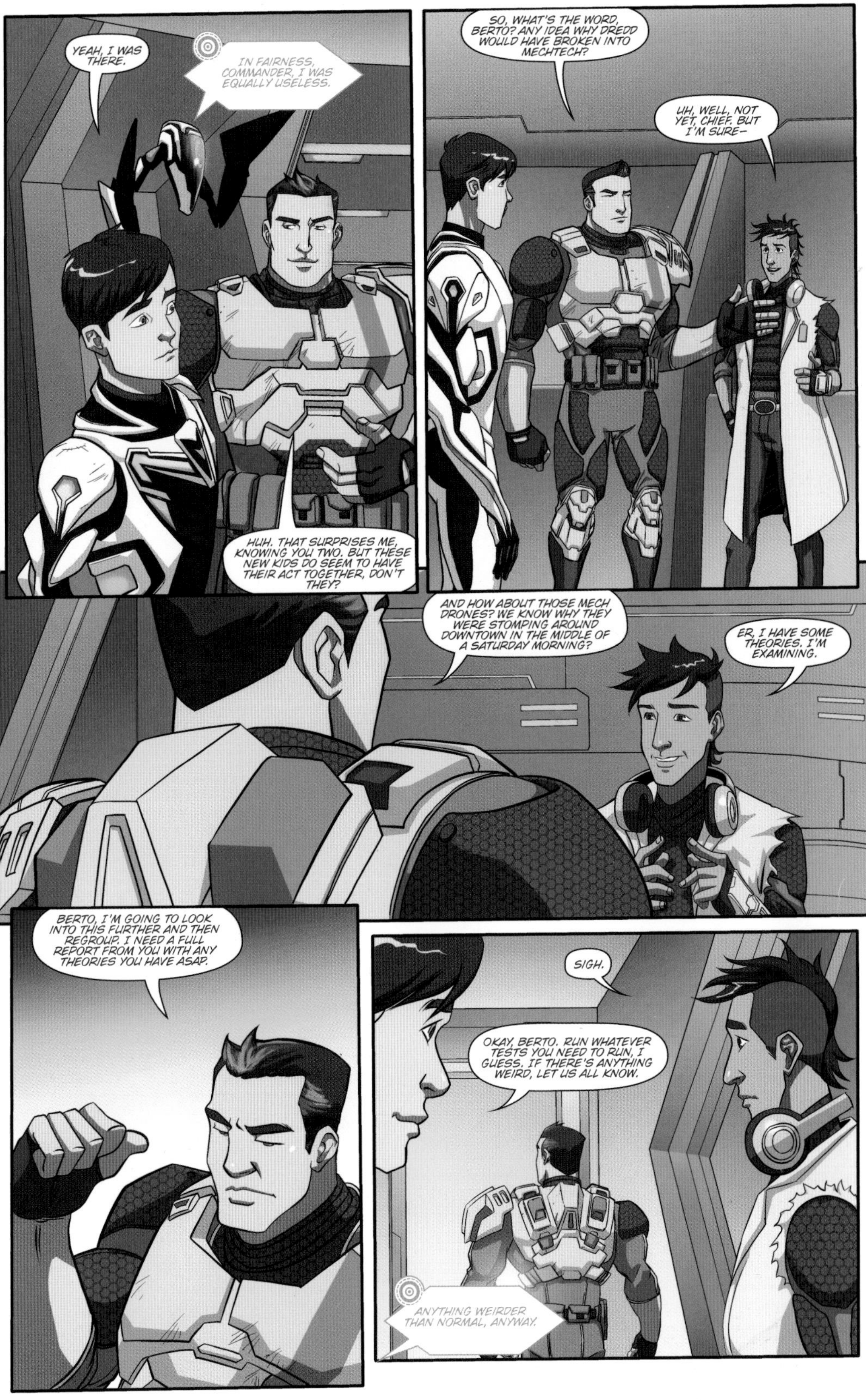
YEAH, I WAS THERE.
IN FAIRNESS, COMMANDER, I WAS EQUALLY USELESS.
HUH. THAT SURPRISES ME, KNOWING YOU TWO. BUT THESE NEW KIDS DO SEEM TO HAVE THEIR ACT TOGETHER, DON'T THEY?
SO, WHAT'S THE WORD, BERTO? ANY IDEA WHY DREDD WOULD HAVE BROKEN INTO MECHTECH?
UH, WELL, NOT YET, CHIEF. BUT I'M SURE—
AND HOW ABOUT THOSE MECH DRONES? WE KNOW WHY THEY WERE STOMPING AROUND DOWNTOWN IN THE MIDDLE OF A SATURDAY MORNING?
ER, I HAVE SOME THEORIES. I'M EXAMINING.
BERTO, I'M GOING TO LOOK INTO THIS FURTHER AND THEN REGROUP. I NEED A FULL REPORT FROM YOU WITH ANY THEORIES YOU HAVE ASAP.
SIGH.
OKAY, BERTO. RUN WHATEVER TESTS YOU NEED TO RUN, I GUESS. IF THERE'S ANYTHING WEIRD, LET US ALL KNOW.
ANYTHING WEIRDER THAN NORMAL, ANYWAY.

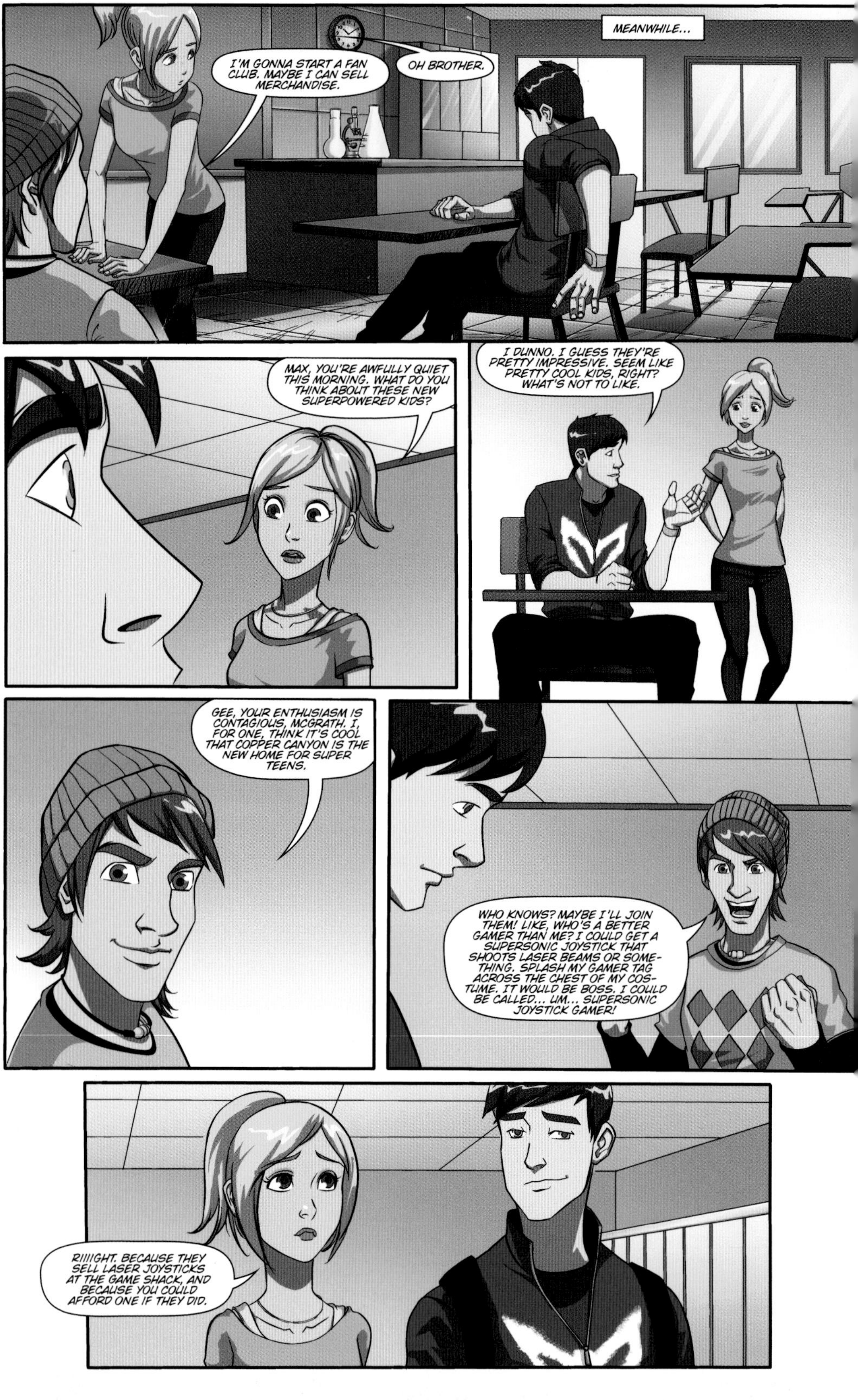
MEANWHILE...
I'M GONNA START A FAN CLUB. MAYBE I CAN SELL MERCHANDISE.
OH BROTHER.
MAX, YOU'RE AWFULLY QUIET THIS MORNING. WHAT DO YOU THINK ABOUT THESE NEW SUPERPOWERED KIDS?
I DUNNO. I GUESS THEY'RE PRETTY IMPRESSIVE. SEEM LIKE PRETTY COOL KIDS, RIGHT? WHAT'S NOT TO LIKE.
GEE, YOUR ENTHUSIASM IS CONTAGIOUS, MCGRATH. I, FOR ONE, THINK IT'S COOL THAT COPPER CANYON IS THE NEW HOME FOR SUPER TEENS.
WHO KNOWS? MAYBE I'LL JOIN THEM! LIKE, WHO'S A BETTER GAMER THAN ME? I COULD GET A SUPERSONIC JOYSTICK THAT SHOOTS LASER BEAMS OR SOME-THING. SPLASH MY GAMER TAG ACROSS THE CHEST OF MY COS-TUME. IT WOULD BE BOSS. I COULD BE CALLED... UM... SUPERSONIC JOYSTICK GAMER!
RIIIIGHT. BECAUSE THEY SELL LASER JOYSTICKS AT THE GAME SHACK, AND BECAUSE YOU COULD AFFORD ONE IF THEY DID.

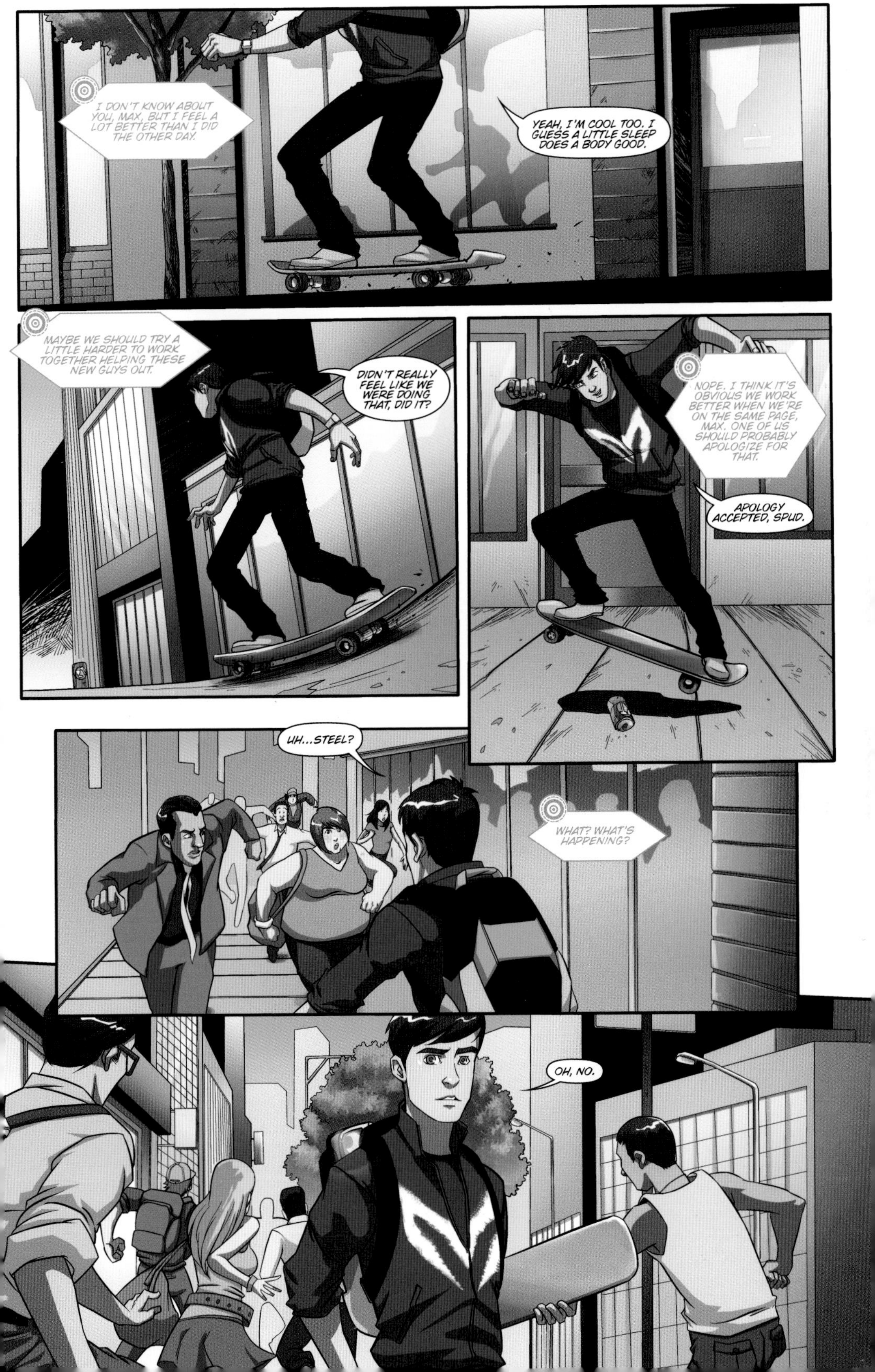
I DON'T KNOW ABOUT YOU, MAX, BUT I FEEL A LOT BETTER THAN I DID THE OTHER DAY.
YEAH, I'M COOL TOO. I GUESS A LITTLE SLEEP DOES A BODY GOOD.
MAYBE WE SHOULD TRY A LITTLE HARDER TO WORK TOGETHER HELPING THESE NEW GUYS OUT.
DIDN'T REALLY FEEL LIKE WE WERE DOING THAT, DID IT?
NOPE. I THINK IT'S OBVIOUS WE WORK BETTER WHEN WE'RE ON THE SAME PAGE, MAX. ONE OF US SHOULD PROBABLY APOLOGIZE FOR THAT.
APOLOGY ACCEPTED, SPUD.
UH...STEEL?
WHAT? WHAT'S HAPPENING?
OH, NO.

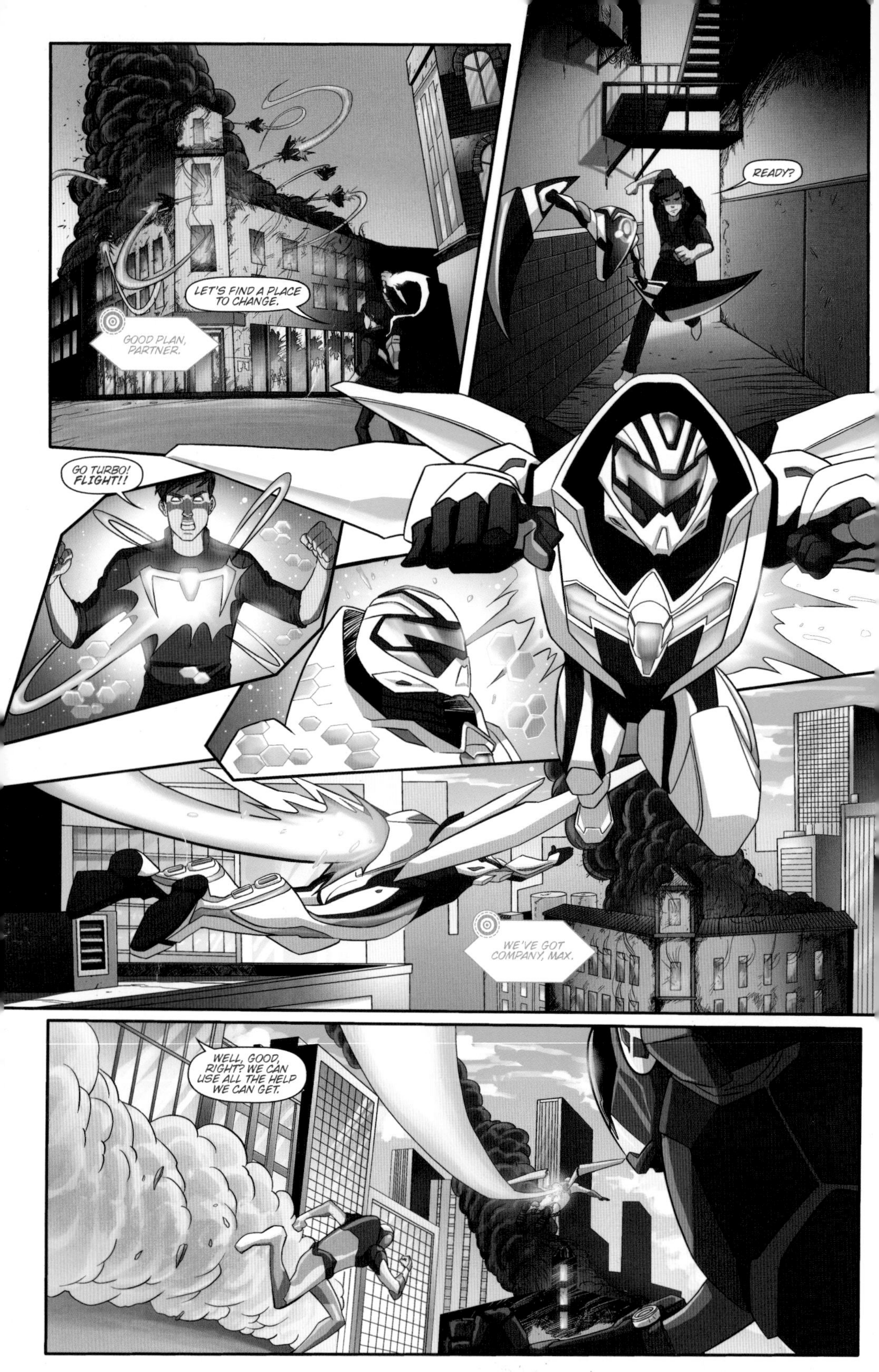
LET'S FIND A PLACE TO CHANGE.
GOOD PLAN, PARTNER.
READY?
GO TURBO! FLIGHT!!
WE'VE GOT COMPANY, MAX.
WELL, GOOD, RIGHT? WE CAN USE ALL THE HELP WE CAN GET.

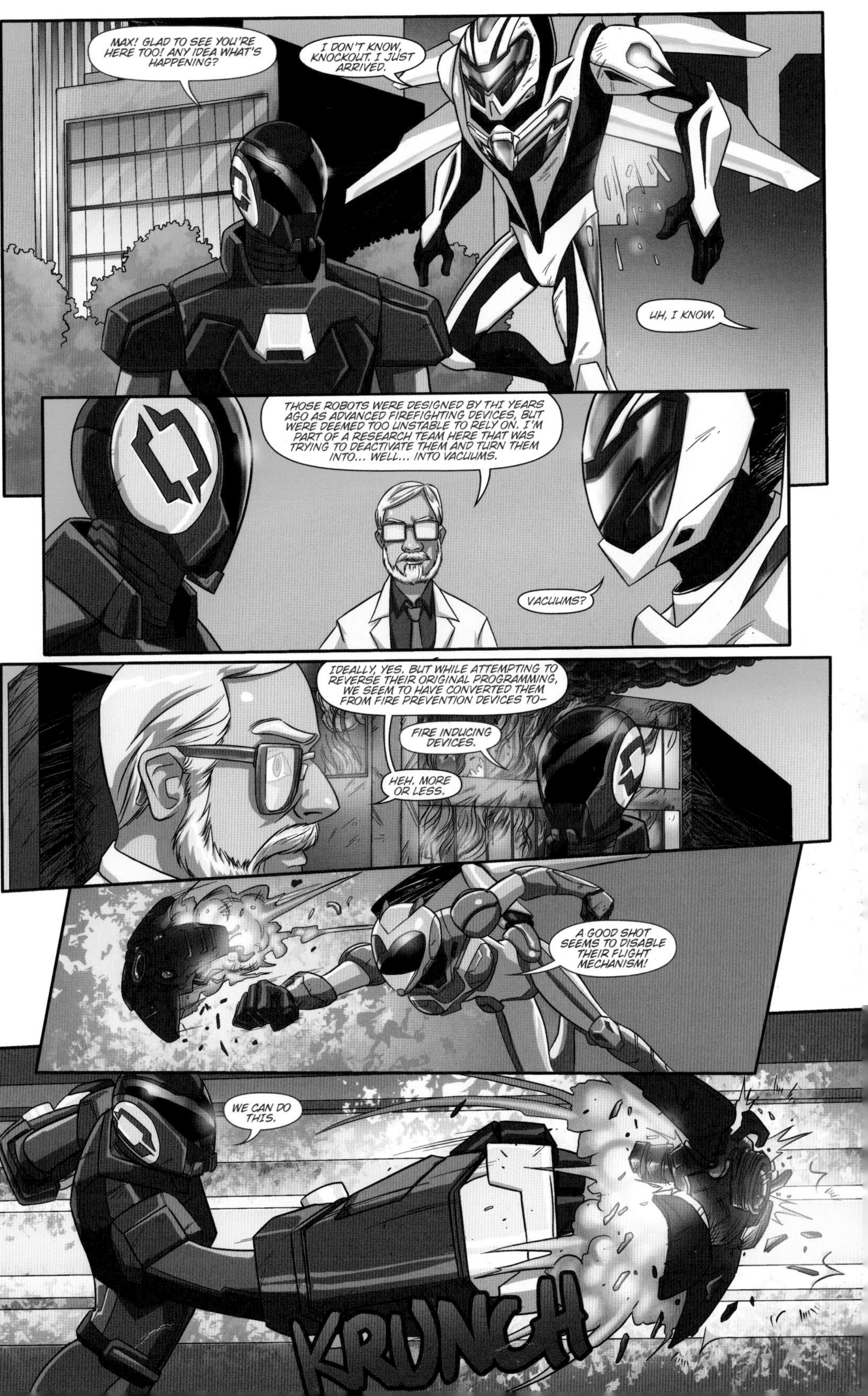
MAX! GLAD TO SEE YOU'RE HERE TOO! ANY IDEA WHAT'S HAPPENING?
I DON'T KNOW, KNOCKOUT. I JUST ARRIVED.
UH, I KNOW.
THOSE ROBOTS WERE DESIGNED BY THI YEARS AGO AS ADVANCED FIREFIGHTING DEVICES, BUT WERE DEEMED TOO UNSTABLE TO RELY ON. I'M PART OF A RESEARCH TEAM HERE THAT WAS TRYING TO DEACTIVATE THEM AND TURN THEM INTO... WELL... INTO VACUUMS.
VACUUMS?
IDEALLY, YES. BUT WHILE ATTEMPTING TO REVERSE THEIR ORIGINAL PROGRAMMING, WE SEEM TO HAVE CONVERTED THEM FROM FIRE PREVENTION DEVICES TO-
FIRE INDUCING DEVICES.
HEH. MORE OR LESS.
A GOOD SHOT SEEMS TO DISABLE THEIR FLIGHT MECHANISM!
WE CAN DO THIS.
KRUNCH

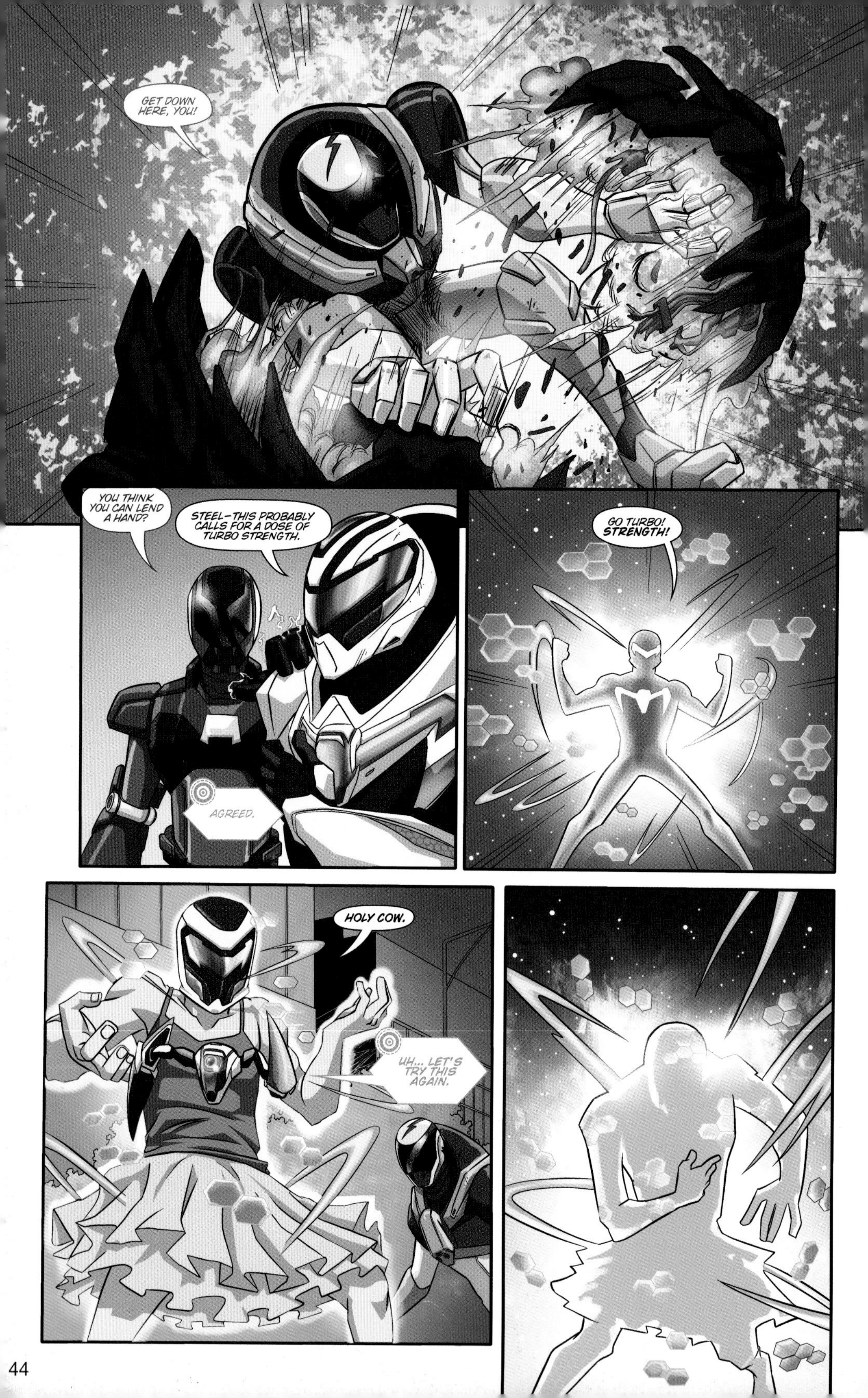
GET DOWN HERE, YOU!
YOU THINK YOU CAN LEND A HAND?
STEEL—THIS PROBABLY CALLS FOR A DOSE OF TURBO STRENGTH.
AGREED.
GO TURBO! STRENGTH!
HOLY COW.
UH... LET'S TRY THIS AGAIN.

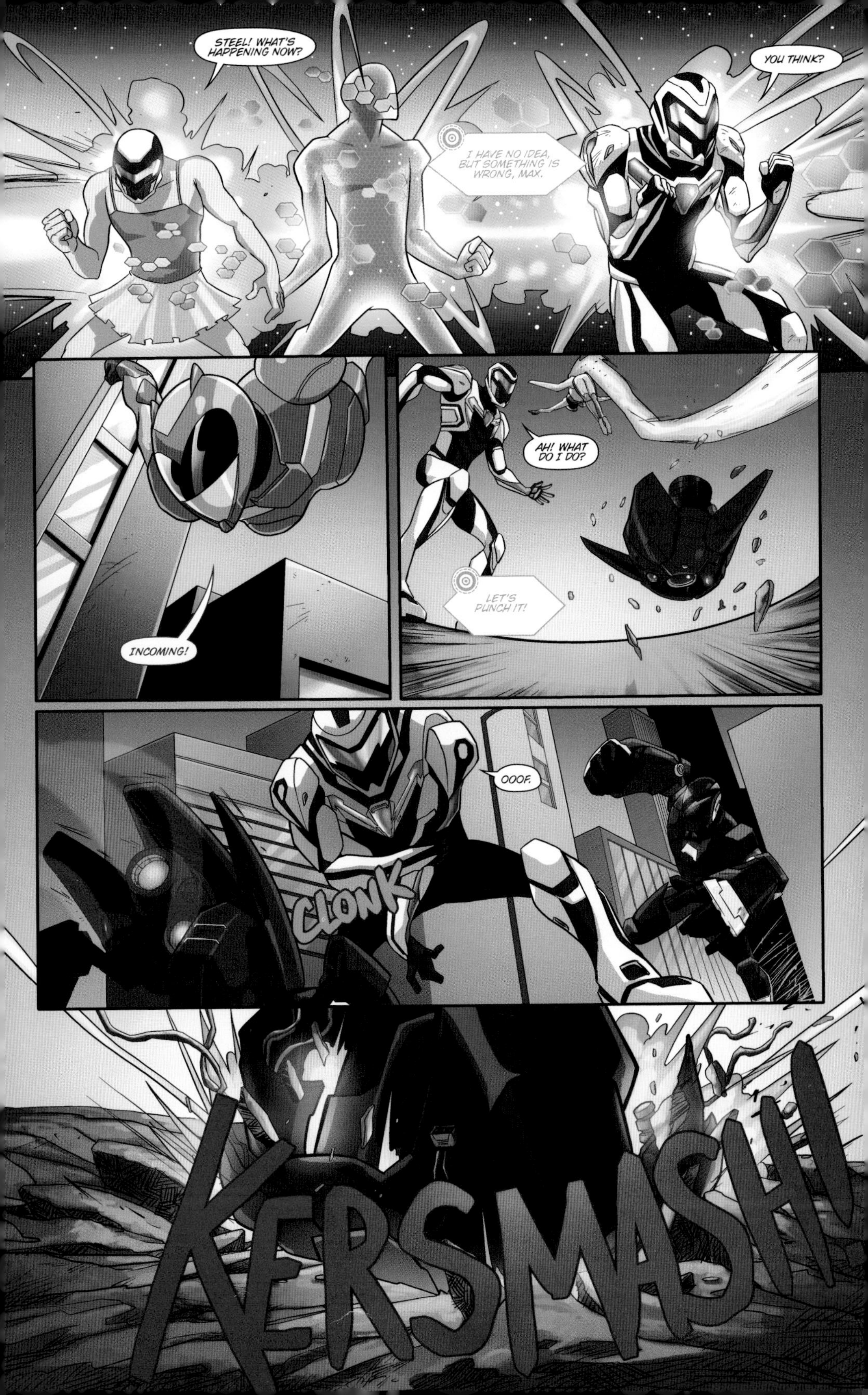
STEEL! WHAT'S HAPPENING NOW?
I HAVE NO IDEA, BUT SOMETHING IS WRONG, MAX.
YOU THINK?
INCOMING!
AH! WHAT DO I DO?
LET'S PUNCH IT!
OOOF.
CLONK
KERSMASH!

CHAPTER 3: POWER DOWN

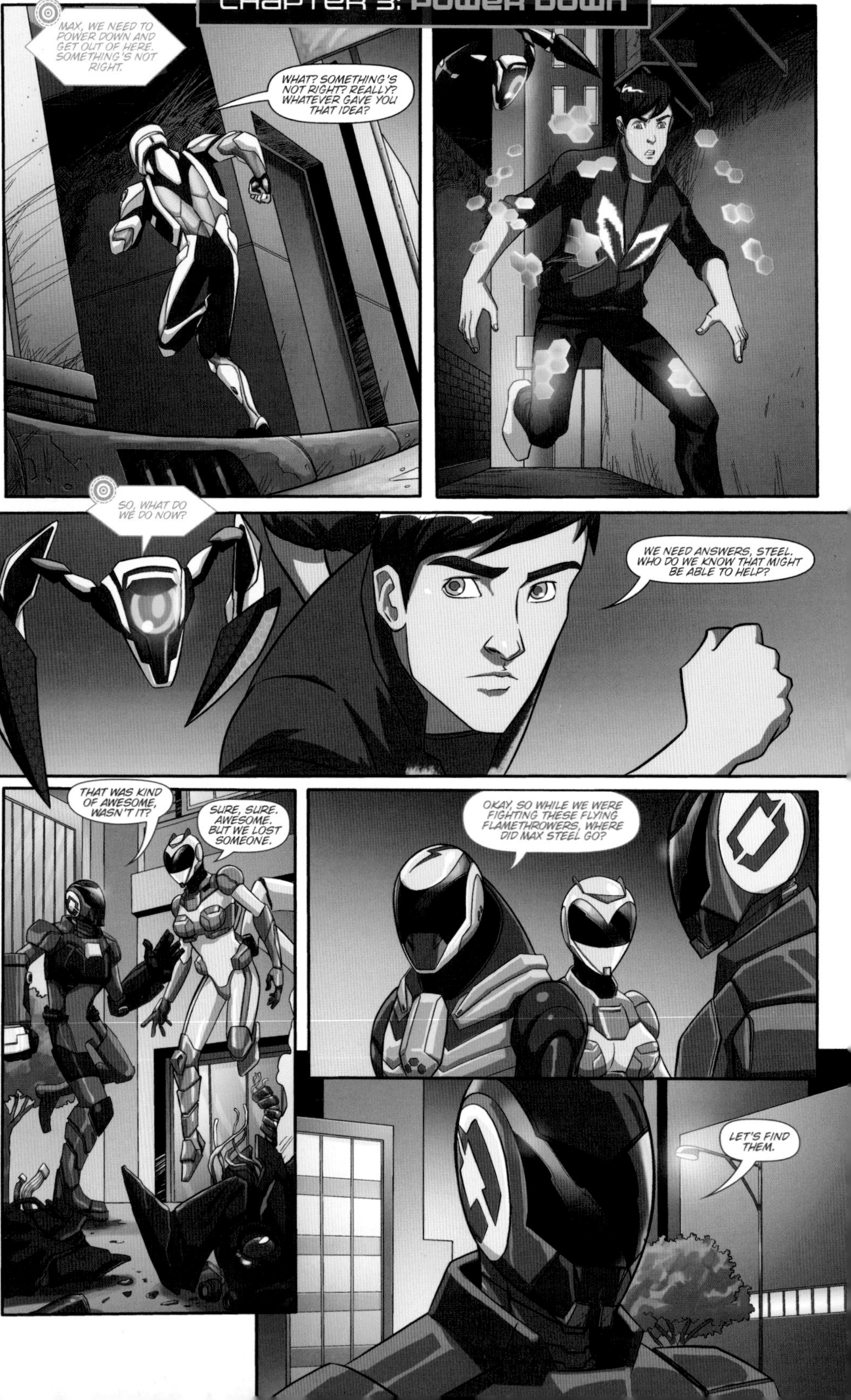
MAX, WE NEED TO POWER DOWN AND GET OUT OF HERE. SOMETHING'S NOT RIGHT.
WHAT? SOMETHING'S NOT RIGHT? REALLY? WHATEVER GAVE YOU THAT IDEA?
SO, WHAT DO WE DO NOW?
WE NEED ANSWERS, STEEL. WHO DO WE KNOW THAT MIGHT BE ABLE TO HELP?
THAT WAS KIND OF AWESOME, WASN'T IT?
SURE, SURE. AWESOME. BUT WE LOST SOMEONE.
OKAY, SO WHILE WE WERE FIGHTING THESE FLYING FLAMETHROWERS, WHERE DID MAX STEEL GO?
LET'S FIND THEM.

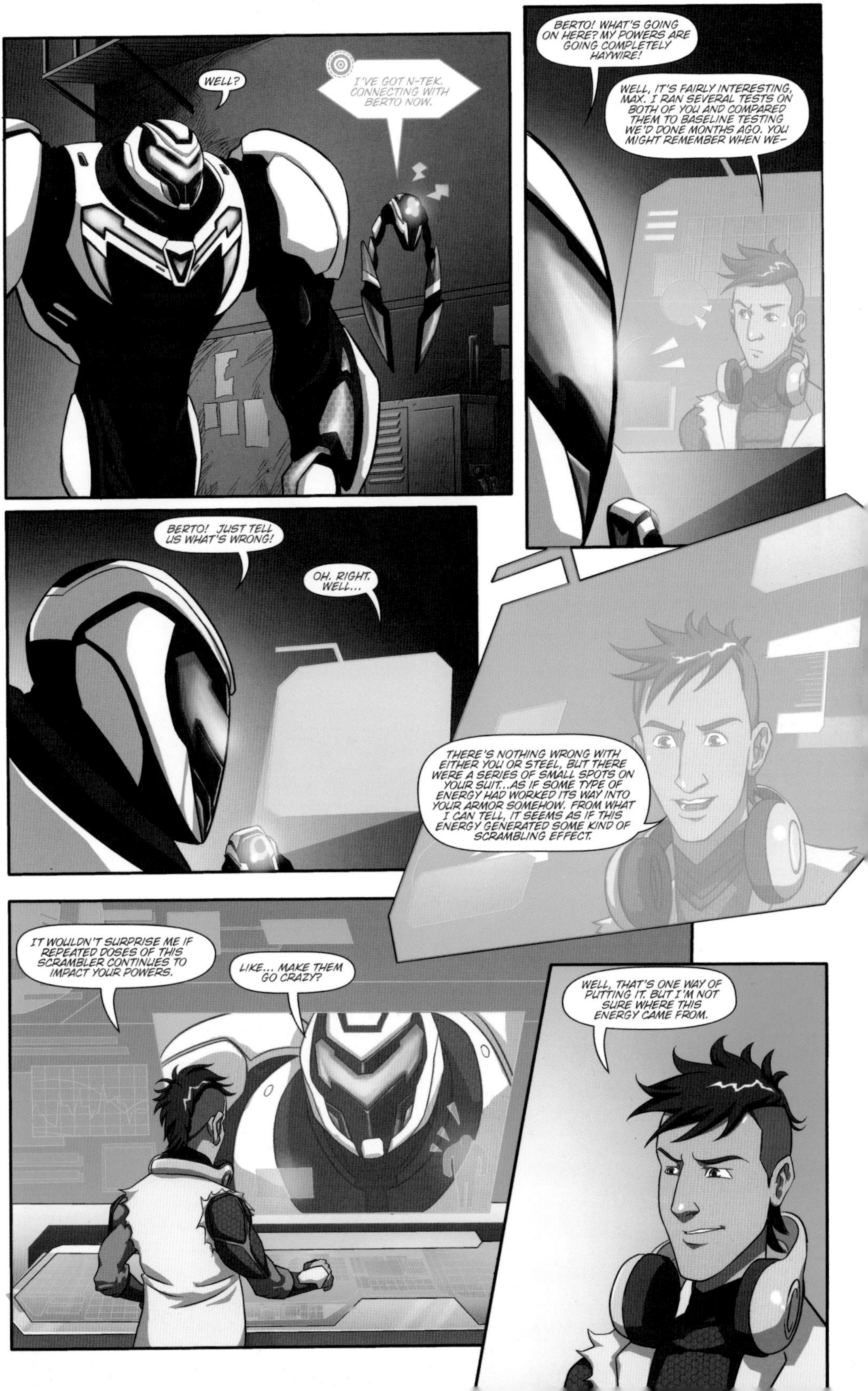
WELL?
I'VE GOT N-TEK. CONNECTING WITH BERTO NOW.
BERTO! WHAT'S GOING ON HERE? MY POWERS ARE GOING COMPLETELY HAYWIRE!
WELL, IT'S FAIRLY INTERESTING, MAX. I RAN SEVERAL TESTS ON BOTH OF YOU AND COMPARED THEM TO BASELINE TESTING WE'D DONE MONTHS AGO. YOU MIGHT REMEMBER WHEN WE-
BERTO! JUST TELL US WHAT'S WRONG!
OH. RIGHT. WELL...
THERE'S NOTHING WRONG WITH EITHER YOU OR STEEL, BUT THERE WERE A SERIES OF SMALL SPOTS ON YOUR SUIT...AS IF SOME TYPE OF ENERGY HAD WORKED ITS WAY INTO YOUR ARMOR SOMEHOW. FROM WHAT I CAN TELL, IT SEEMS AS IF THIS ENERGY GENERATED SOME KIND OF SCRAMBLING EFFECT.
IT WOULDN'T SURPRISE ME IF REPEATED DOSES OF THIS SCRAMBLER CONTINUES TO IMPACT YOUR POWERS.
LIKE... MAKE THEM GO CRAZY?
WELL, THAT'S ONE WAY OF PUTTING IT. BUT I'M NOT SURE WHERE THIS ENERGY CAME FROM.

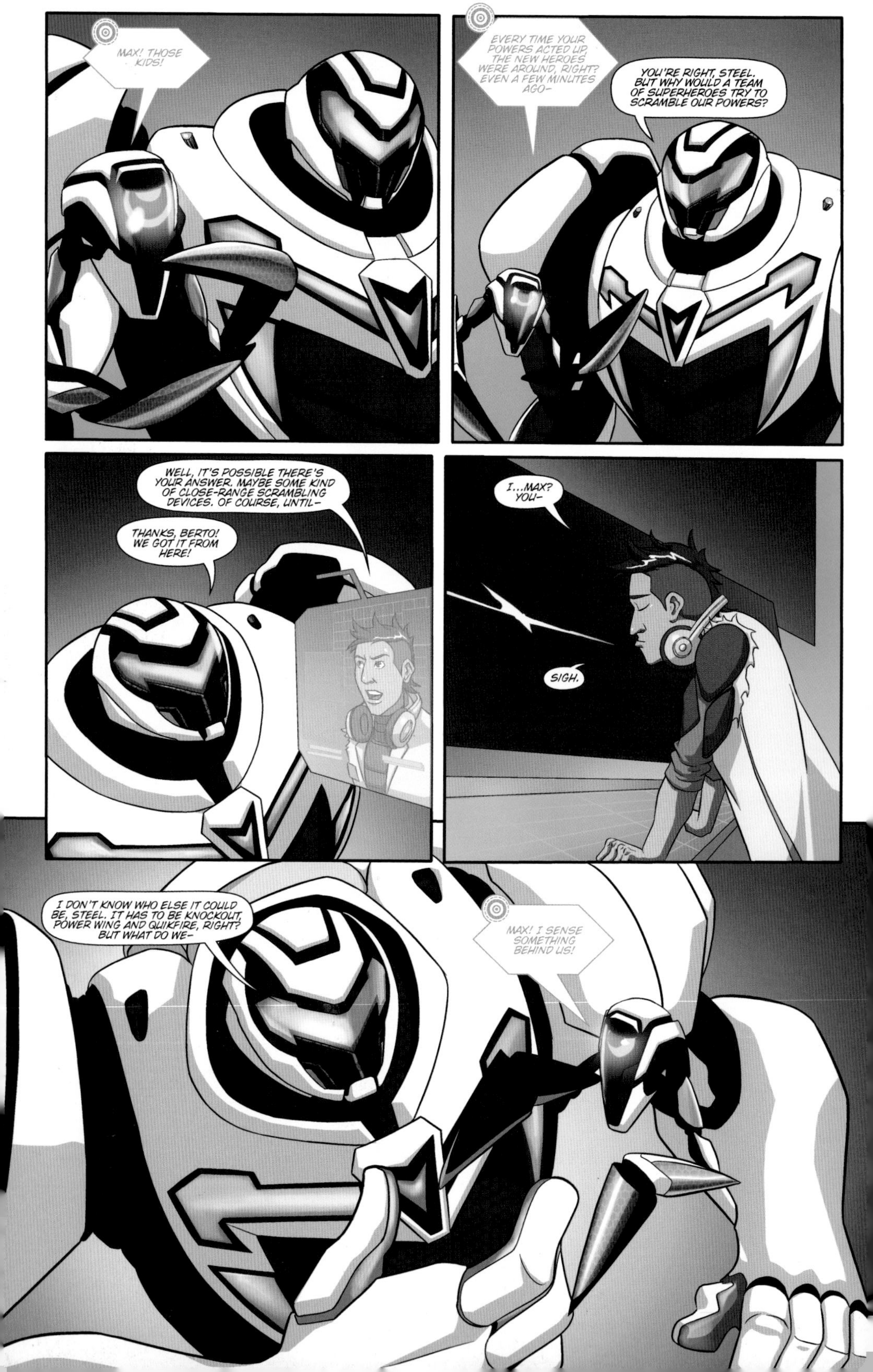
MAX! THOSE KIDS!
EVERY TIME YOUR POWERS ACTED UP, THE NEW HEROES WERE AROUND, RIGHT? EVEN A FEW MINUTES AGO–
YOU'RE RIGHT, STEEL. BUT WHY WOULD A TEAM OF SUPERHEROES TRY TO SCRAMBLE OUR POWERS?
WELL, IT'S POSSIBLE THERE'S YOUR ANSWER. MAYBE SOME KIND OF CLOSE-RANGE SCRAMBLING DEVICES. OF COURSE, UNTIL–
THANKS, BERTO! WE GOT IT FROM HERE!
I...MAX? YOU–
SIGH.
I DON'T KNOW WHO ELSE IT COULD BE, STEEL. IT HAS TO BE KNOCKOUT, POWER WING AND QUIKFIRE, RIGHT? BUT WHAT DO WE–
MAX! I SENSE SOMETHING BEHIND US!

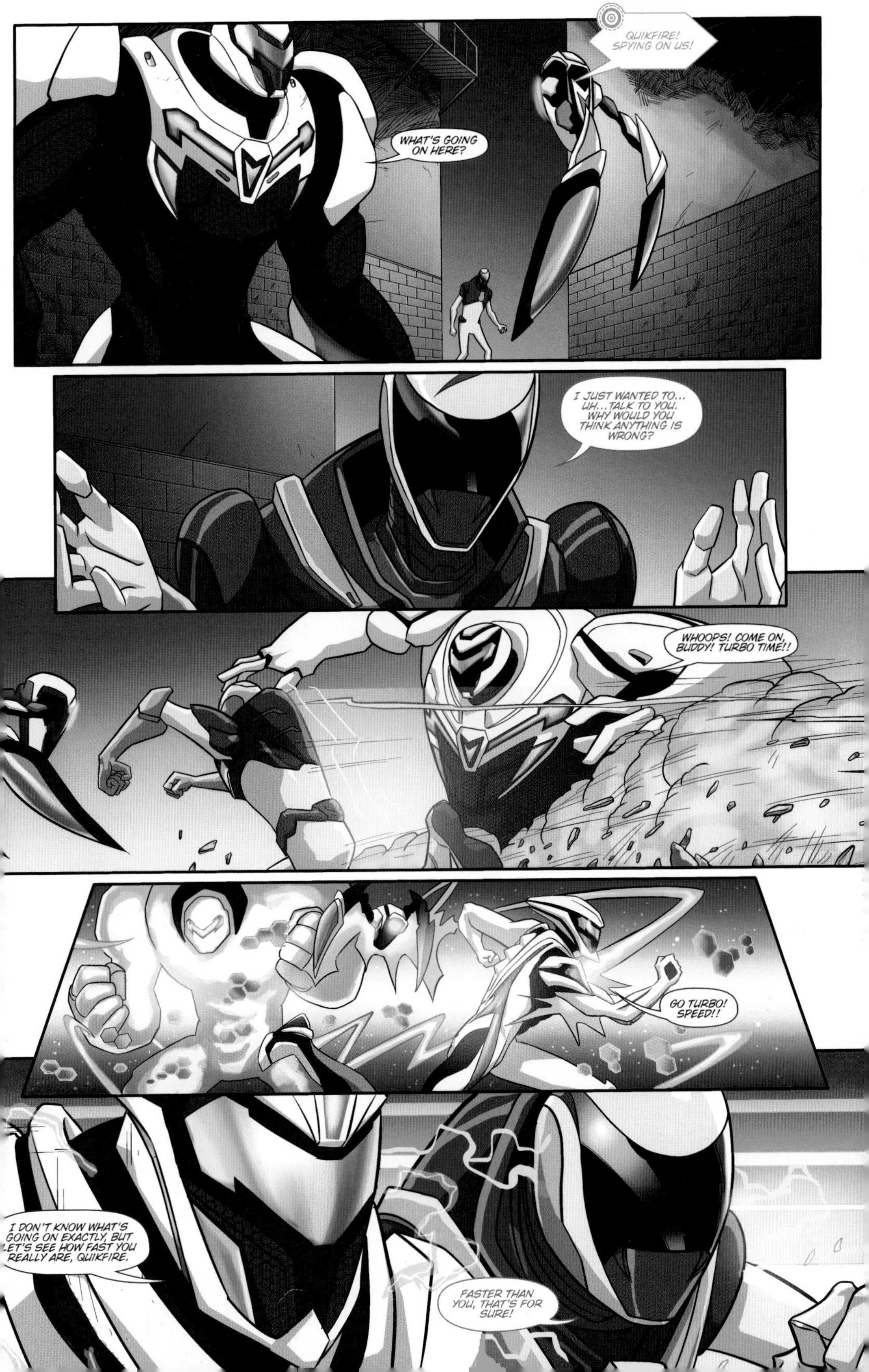
WHAT'S GOING ON HERE?
QUIKFIRE! SPYING ON US!
I JUST WANTED TO... UH...TALK TO YOU. WHY WOULD YOU THINK ANYTHING IS WRONG?
WHOOPS! COME ON, BUDDY! TURBO TIME!!
GO TURBO! SPEED!!
I DON'T KNOW WHAT'S GOING ON EXACTLY, BUT LET'S SEE HOW FAST YOU REALLY ARE, QUIKFIRE.
FASTER THAN YOU, THAT'S FOR SURE!

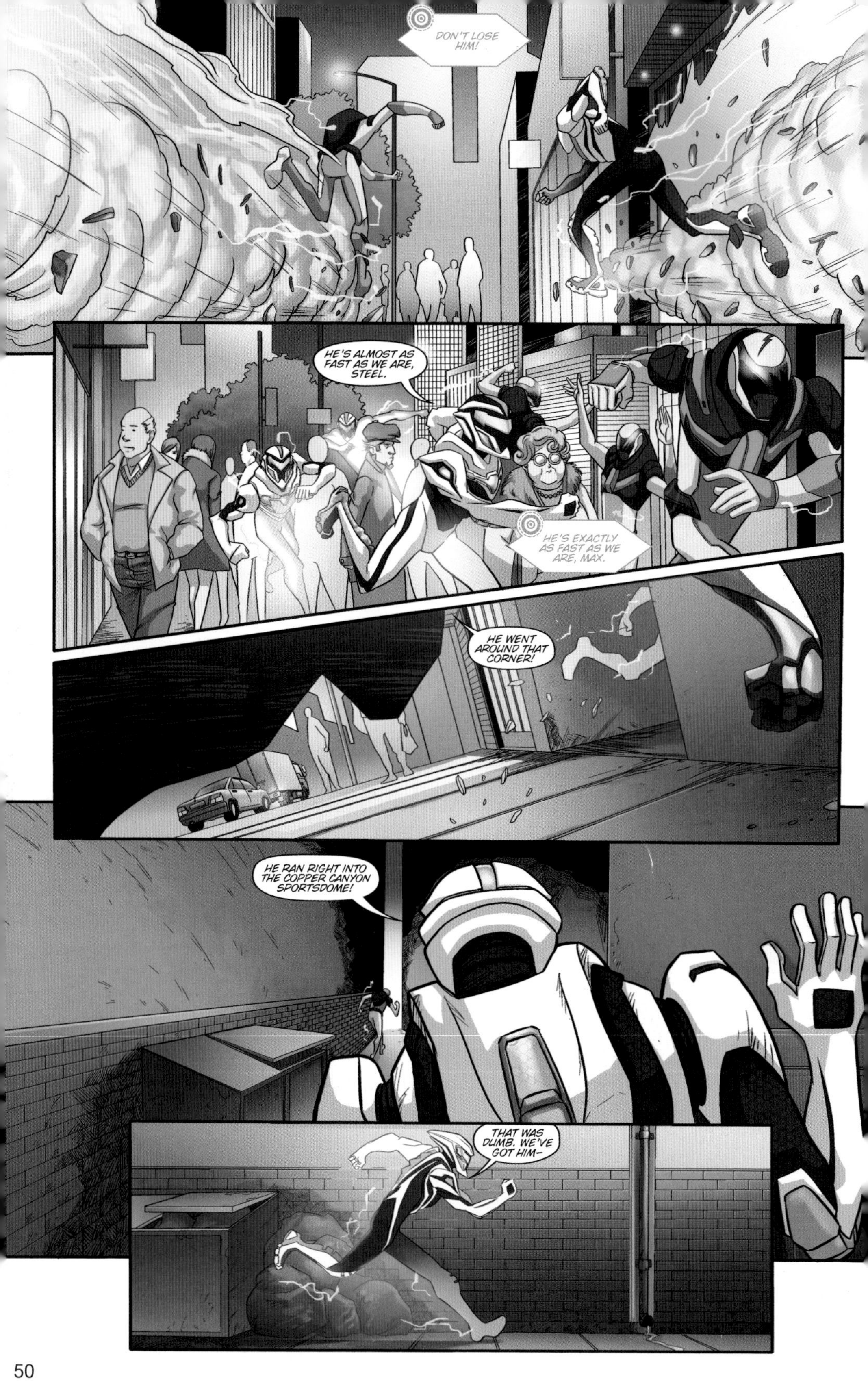
DON'T LOSE HIM!
HE'S ALMOST AS FAST AS WE ARE, STEEL.
HE'S EXACTLY AS FAST AS WE ARE, MAX.
HE WENT AROUND THAT CORNER!
HE RAN RIGHT INTO THE COPPER CANYON SPORTSDOME!
THAT WAS DUMB. WE'VE GOT HIM-

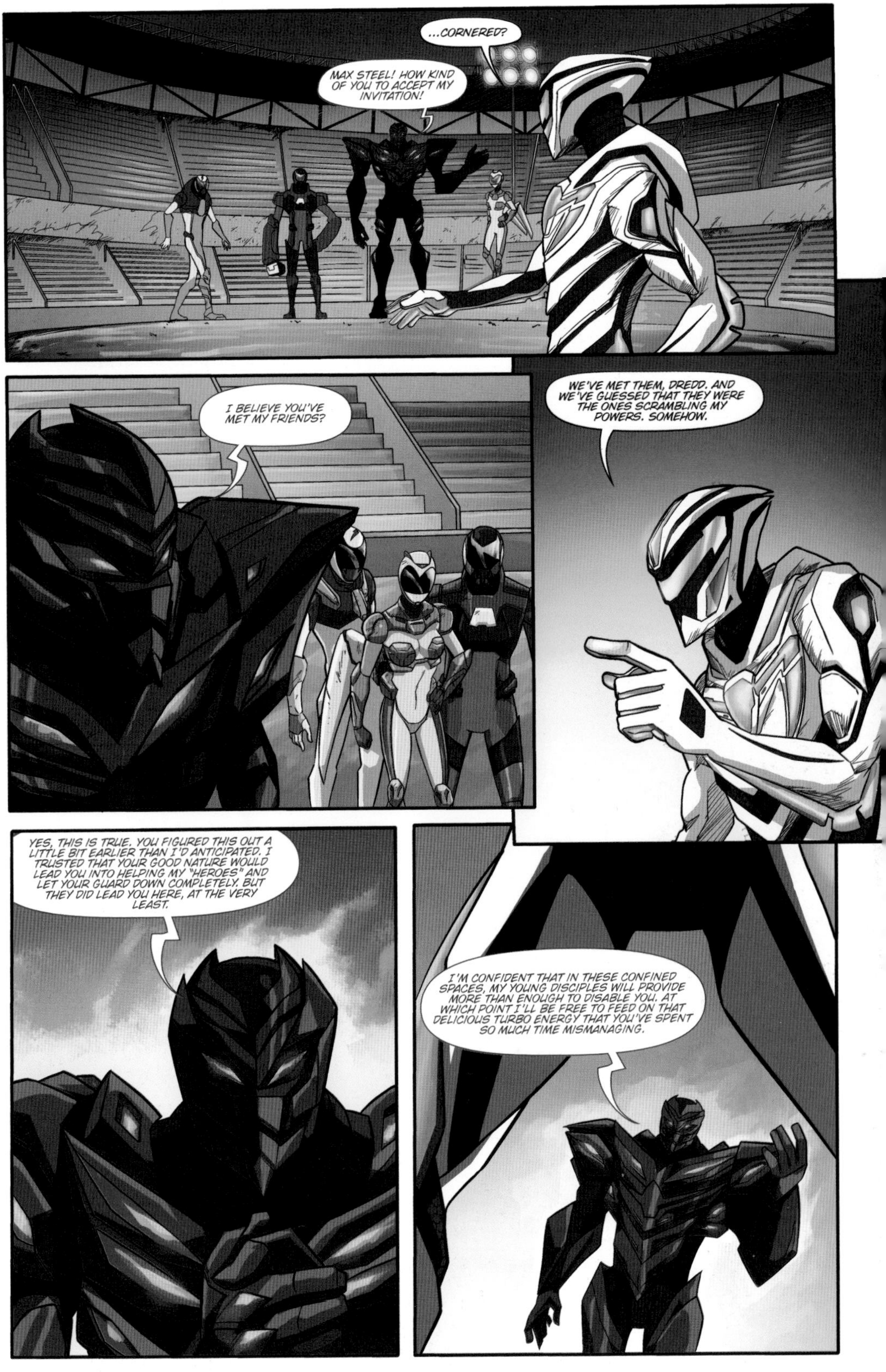
...CORNERED?
MAX STEEL! HOW KIND OF YOU TO ACCEPT MY INVITATION!
I BELIEVE YOU'VE MET MY FRIENDS?
WE'VE MET THEM, DREDD. AND WE'VE GUESSED THAT THEY WERE THE ONES SCRAMBLING MY POWERS. SOMEHOW.
YES, THIS IS TRUE. YOU FIGURED THIS OUT A LITTLE BIT EARLIER THAN I'D ANTICIPATED. I TRUSTED THAT YOUR GOOD NATURE WOULD LEAD YOU INTO HELPING MY "HEROES" AND LET YOUR GUARD DOWN COMPLETELY. BUT THEY DID LEAD YOU HERE, AT THE VERY LEAST.
I'M CONFIDENT THAT IN THESE CONFINED SPACES, MY YOUNG DISCIPLES WILL PROVIDE MORE THAN ENOUGH TO DISABLE YOU. AT WHICH POINT I'LL BE FREE TO FEED ON THAT DELICIOUS TURBO ENERGY THAT YOU'VE SPENT SO MUCH TIME MISMANAGING.

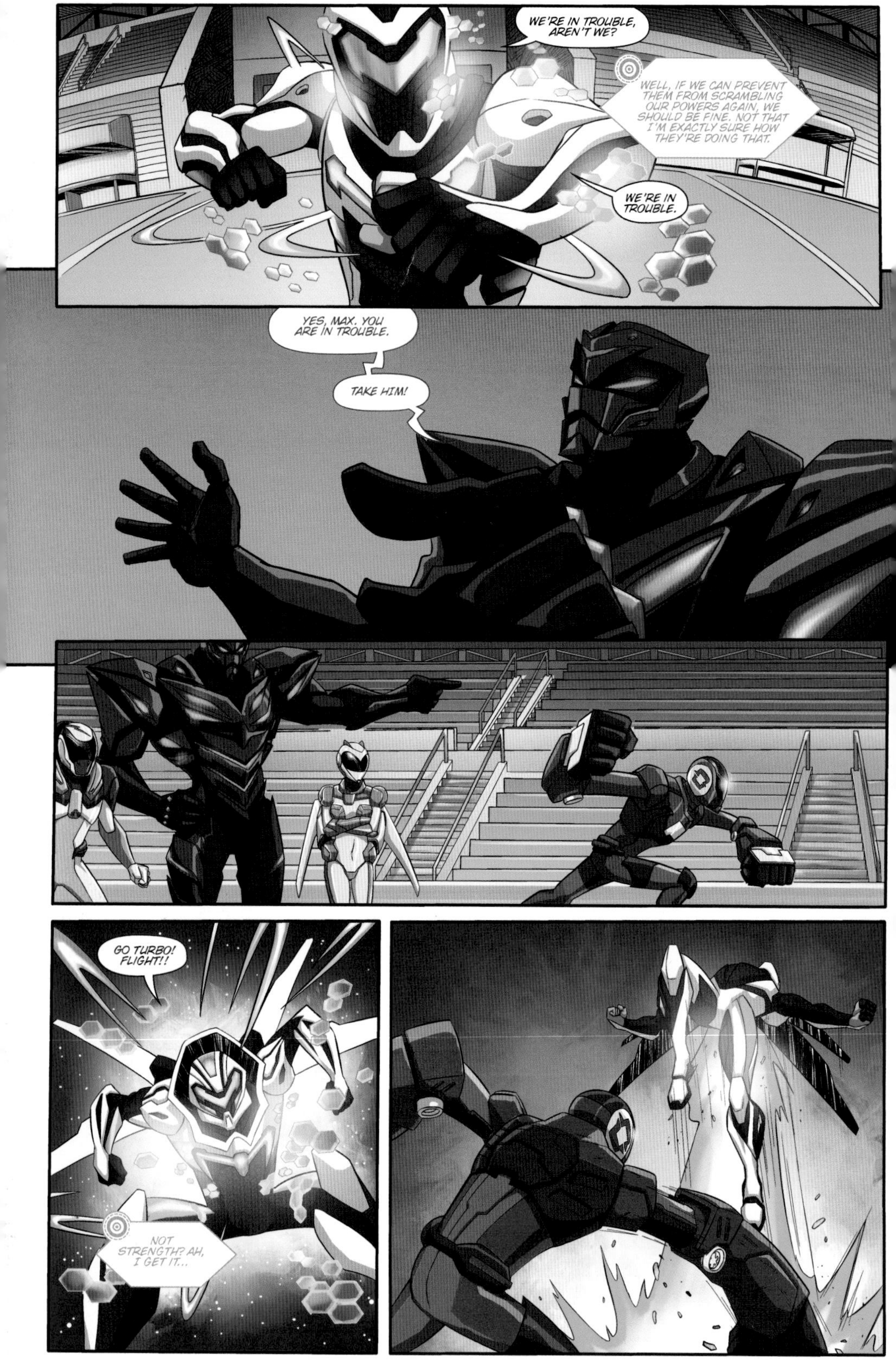
WE'RE IN TROUBLE, AREN'T WE?
WELL, IF WE CAN PREVENT THEM FROM SCRAMBLING OUR POWERS AGAIN, WE SHOULD BE FINE. NOT THAT I'M EXACTLY SURE HOW THEY'RE DOING THAT.
WE'RE IN TROUBLE.
YES, MAX. YOU ARE IN TROUBLE.
TAKE HIM!
GO TURBO! FLIGHT!!
NOT STRENGTH? AH, I GET IT...

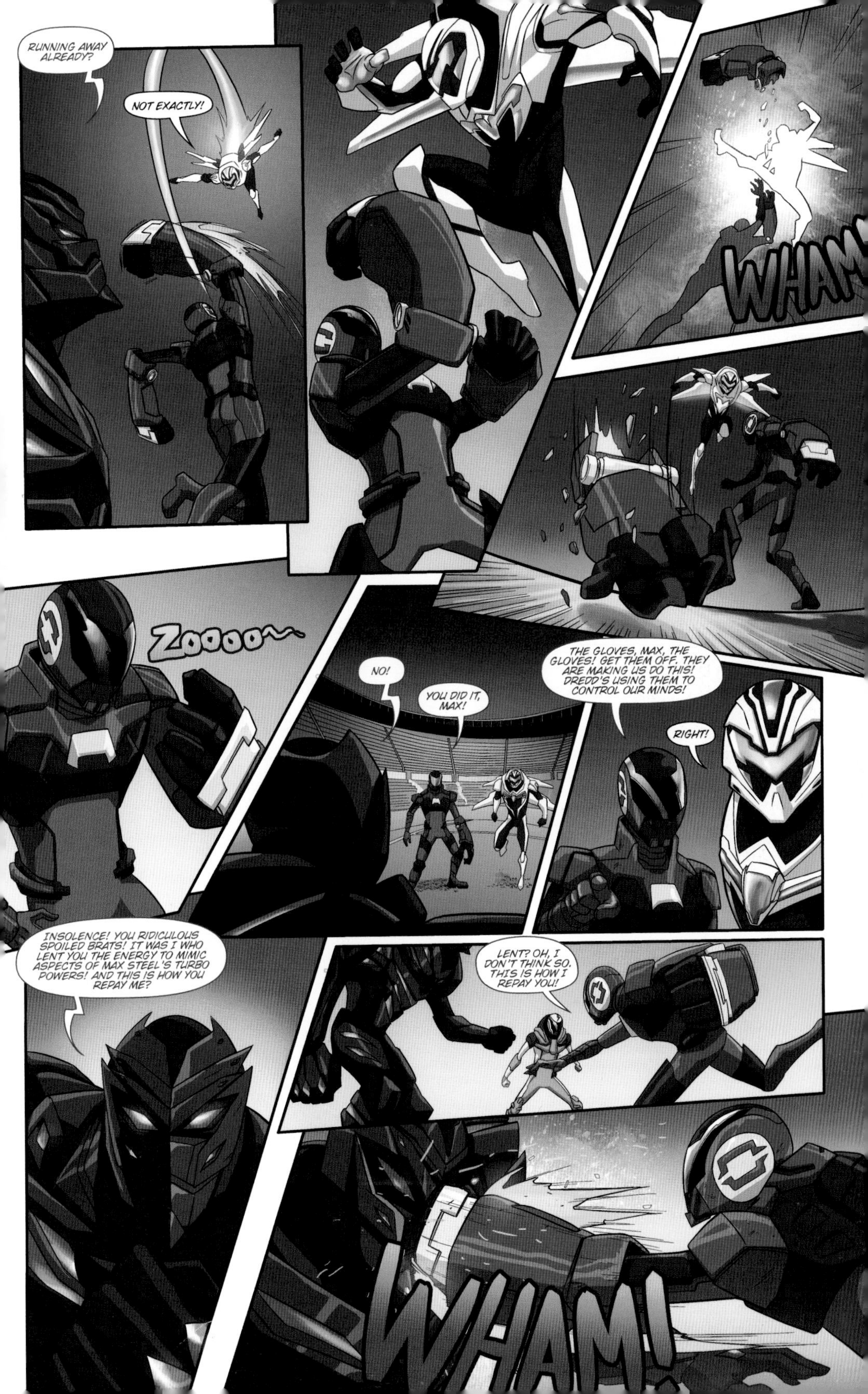
RUNNING AWAY ALREADY?
NOT EXACTLY!
WHAM
ZOOOO
NO!
YOU DID IT, MAX!
THE GLOVES, MAX, THE GLOVES! GET THEM OFF. THEY ARE MAKING US DO THIS! DREDD'S USING THEM TO CONTROL OUR MINDS!
RIGHT!
INSOLENCE! YOU RIDICULOUS SPOILED BRATS! IT WAS I WHO LENT YOU THE ENERGY TO MIMIC ASPECTS OF MAX STEEL'S TURBO POWERS! AND THIS IS HOW YOU REPAY ME?
LENT? OH, I DON'T THINK SO. THIS IS HOW I REPAY YOU!
WHAM!

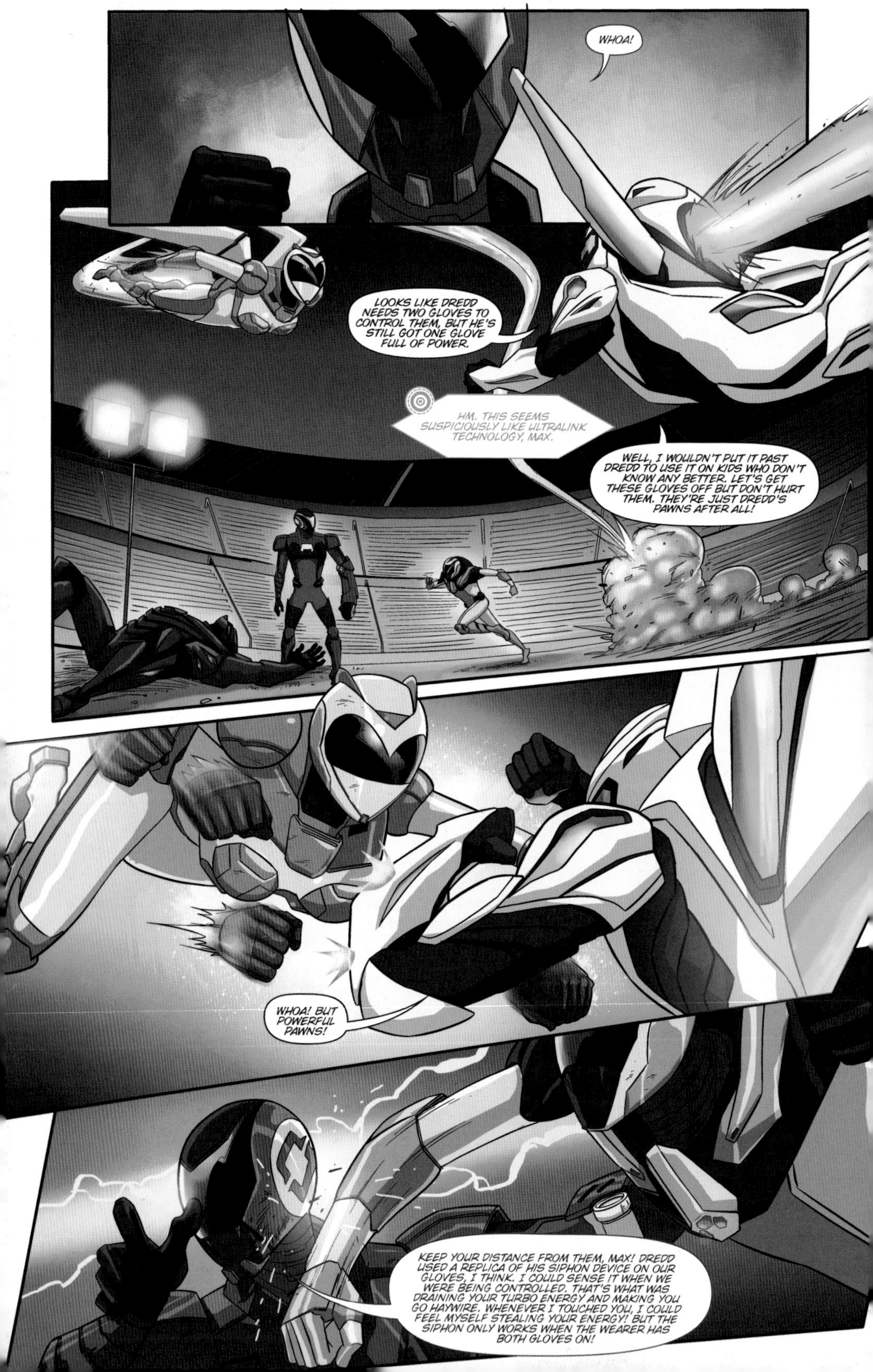
WHOA!
LOOKS LIKE DREDD NEEDS TWO GLOVES TO CONTROL THEM, BUT HE'S STILL GOT ONE GLOVE FULL OF POWER.
HM. THIS SEEMS SUSPICIOUSLY LIKE ULTRALINK TECHNOLOGY, MAX.
WELL, I WOULDN'T PUT IT PAST DREDD TO USE IT ON KIDS WHO DON'T KNOW ANY BETTER. LET'S GET THESE GLOVES OFF BUT DON'T HURT THEM. THEY'RE JUST DREDD'S PAWNS AFTER ALL!
WHOA! BUT POWERFUL PAWNS!
KEEP YOUR DISTANCE FROM THEM, MAX! DREDD USED A REPLICA OF HIS SIPHON DEVICE ON OUR GLOVES, I THINK. I COULD SENSE IT WHEN WE WERE BEING CONTROLLED. THAT'S WHAT WAS DRAINING YOUR TURBO ENERGY AND MAKING YOU GO HAYWIRE. WHENEVER I TOUCHED YOU, I COULD FEEL MYSELF STEALING YOUR ENERGY! BUT THE SIPHON ONLY WORKS WHEN THE WEARER HAS BOTH GLOVES ON!

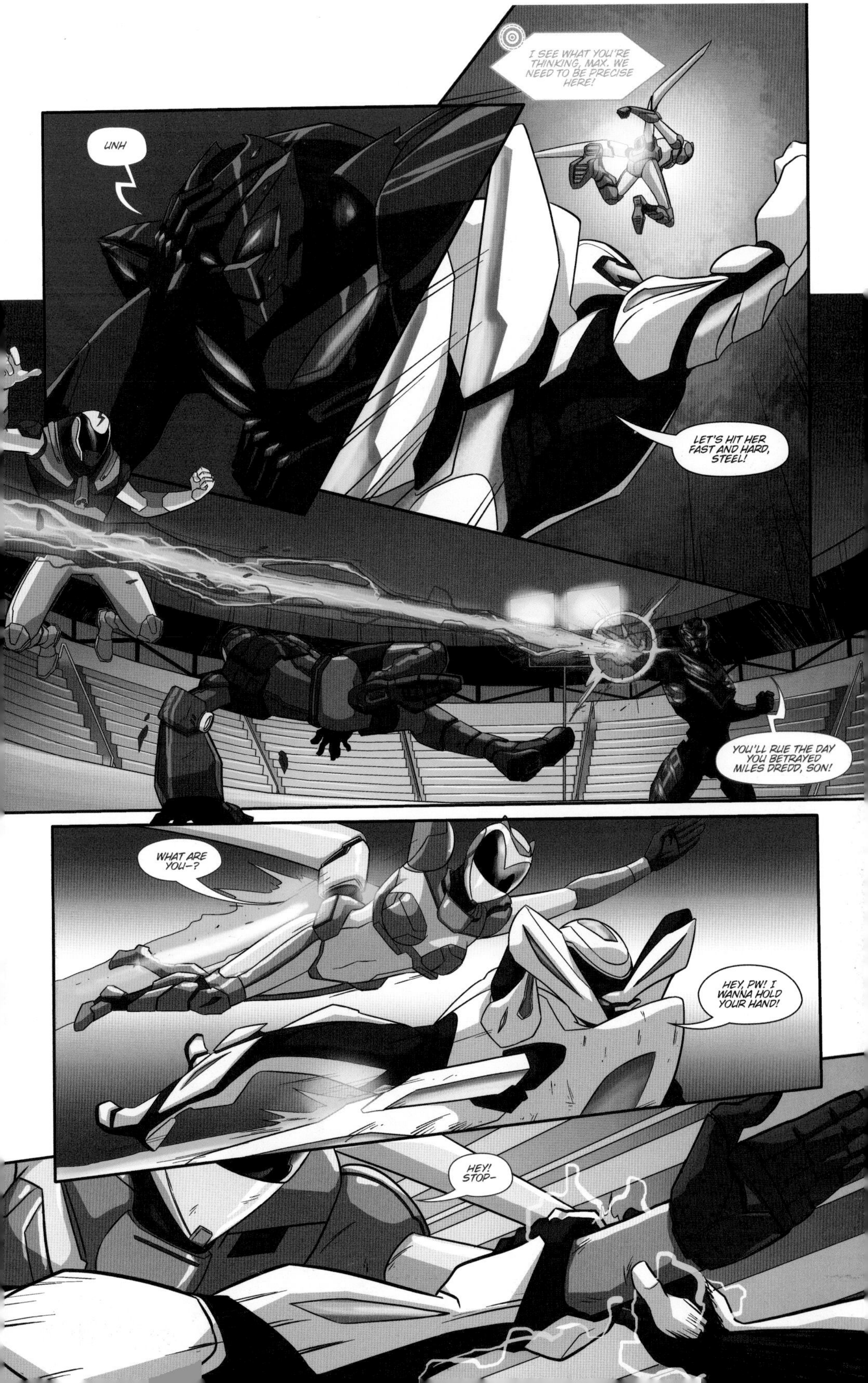
I SEE WHAT YOU'RE THINKING, MAX. WE NEED TO BE PRECISE HERE!
UNH
LET'S HIT HER FAST AND HARD, STEEL!
YOU'LL RUE THE DAY YOU BETRAYED MILES DREDD, SON!
WHAT ARE YOU-?
HEY, PW! I WANNA HOLD YOUR HAND!
HEY! STOP-

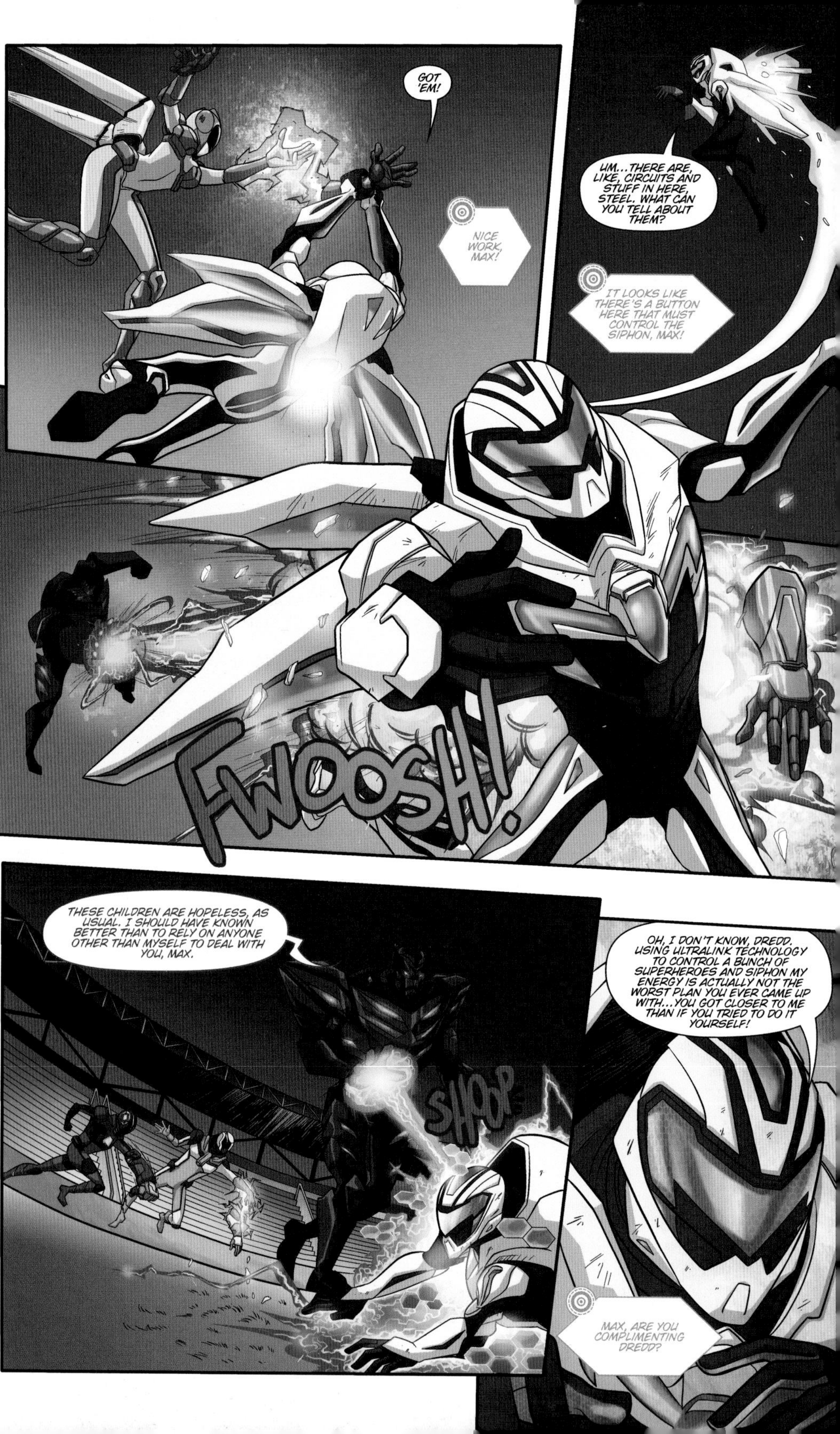
GOT 'EM!
NICE WORK, MAX!
UM...THERE ARE, LIKE, CIRCUITS AND STUFF IN HERE, STEEL. WHAT CAN YOU TELL ABOUT THEM?
IT LOOKS LIKE THERE'S A BUTTON HERE THAT MUST CONTROL THE SIPHON, MAX!
FWOOSH!
THESE CHILDREN ARE HOPELESS, AS USUAL. I SHOULD HAVE KNOWN BETTER THAN TO RELY ON ANYONE OTHER THAN MYSELF TO DEAL WITH YOU, MAX.
SHOOP
OH, I DON'T KNOW, DREDD. USING ULTRALINK TECHNOLOGY TO CONTROL A BUNCH OF SUPERHEROES AND SIPHON MY ENERGY IS ACTUALLY NOT THE WORST PLAN YOU EVER CAME UP WITH...YOU GOT CLOSER TO ME THAN IF YOU TRIED TO DO IT YOURSELF!
MAX, ARE YOU COMPLIMENTING DREDD?

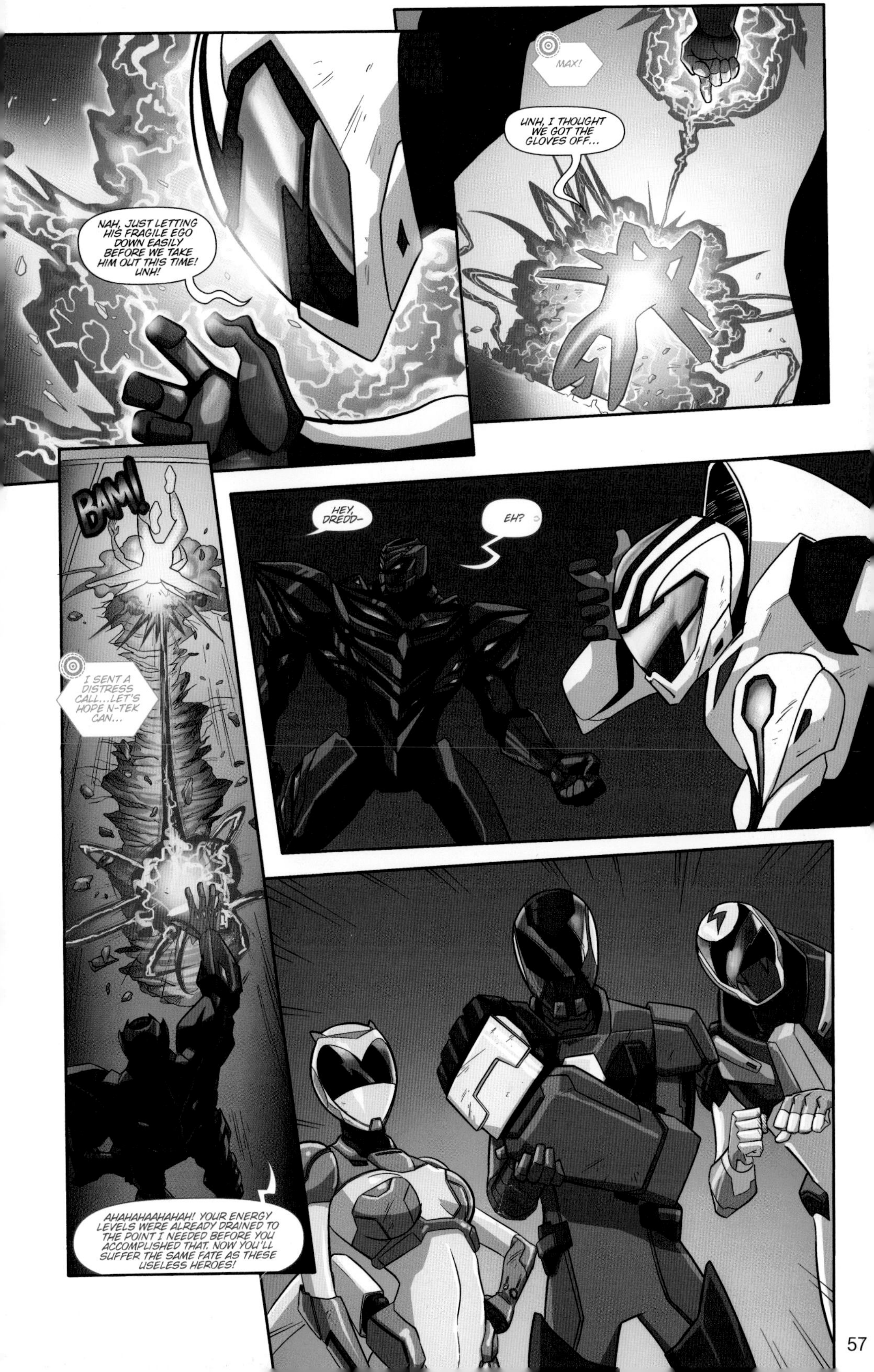
NAH, JUST LETTING HIS FRAGILE EGO DOWN EASILY BEFORE WE TAKE HIM OUT THIS TIME! UNH!
MAX!
UNH, I THOUGHT WE GOT THE GLOVES OFF...
BAM!
I SENT A DISTRESS CALL...LET'S HOPE N-TEK CAN...
HEY, DREDD--
EH?
AHAHAHAAHAHAH! YOUR ENERGY LEVELS WERE ALREADY DRAINED TO THE POINT I NEEDED BEFORE YOU ACCOMPLISHED THAT. NOW YOU'LL SUFFER THE SAME FATE AS THESE USELESS HEROES!

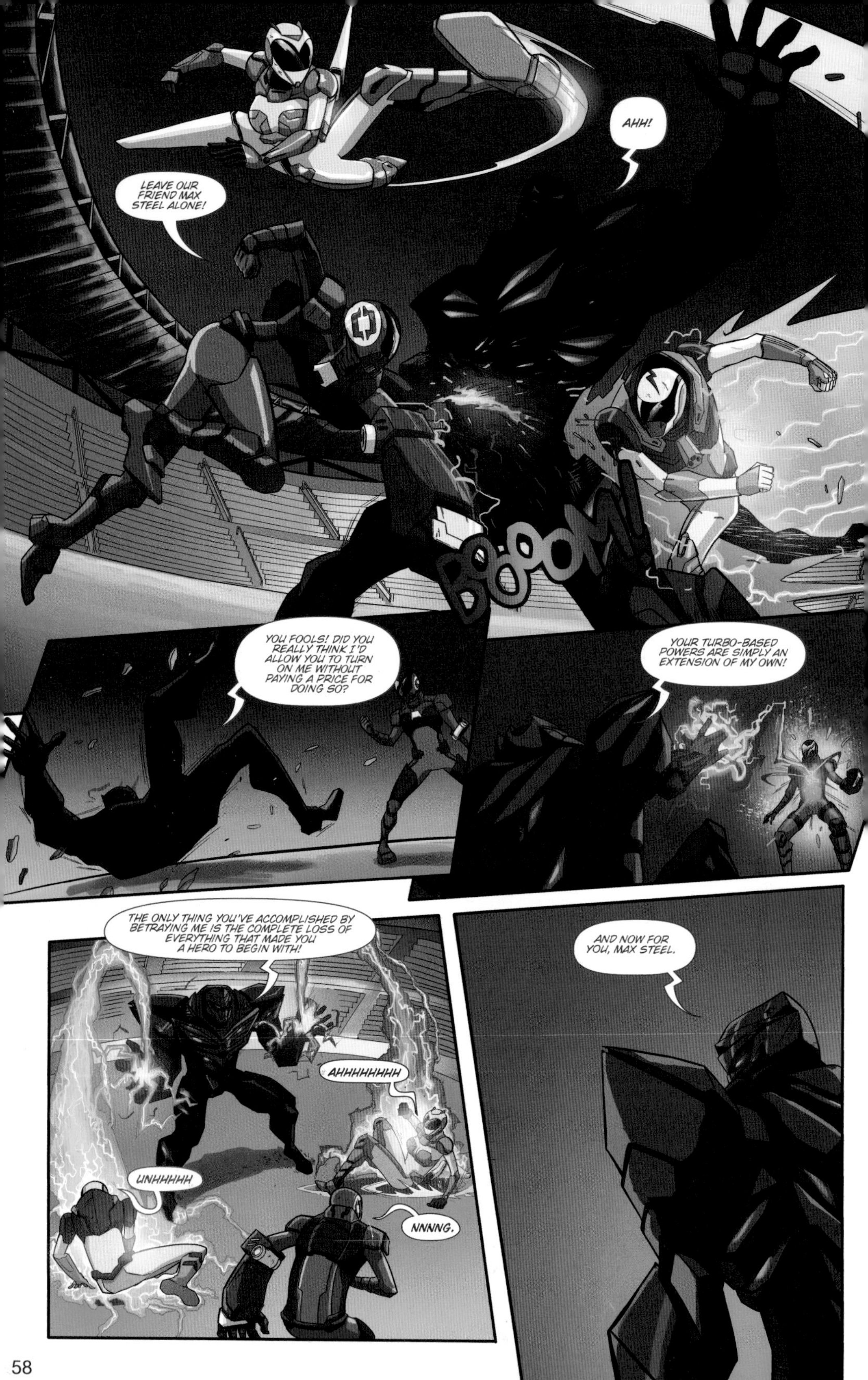
LEAVE OUR FRIEND MAX STEEL ALONE!
AHH!
BOOOM!
YOU FOOLS! DID YOU REALLY THINK I'D ALLOW YOU TO TURN ON ME WITHOUT PAYING A PRICE FOR DOING SO?
YOUR TURBO-BASED POWERS ARE SIMPLY AN EXTENSION OF MY OWN!
THE ONLY THING YOU'VE ACCOMPLISHED BY BETRAYING ME IS THE COMPLETE LOSS OF EVERYTHING THAT MADE YOU A HERO TO BEGIN WITH!
AHHHHHHHH
UNHHHHH
NNNNG.
AND NOW FOR YOU, MAX STEEL.

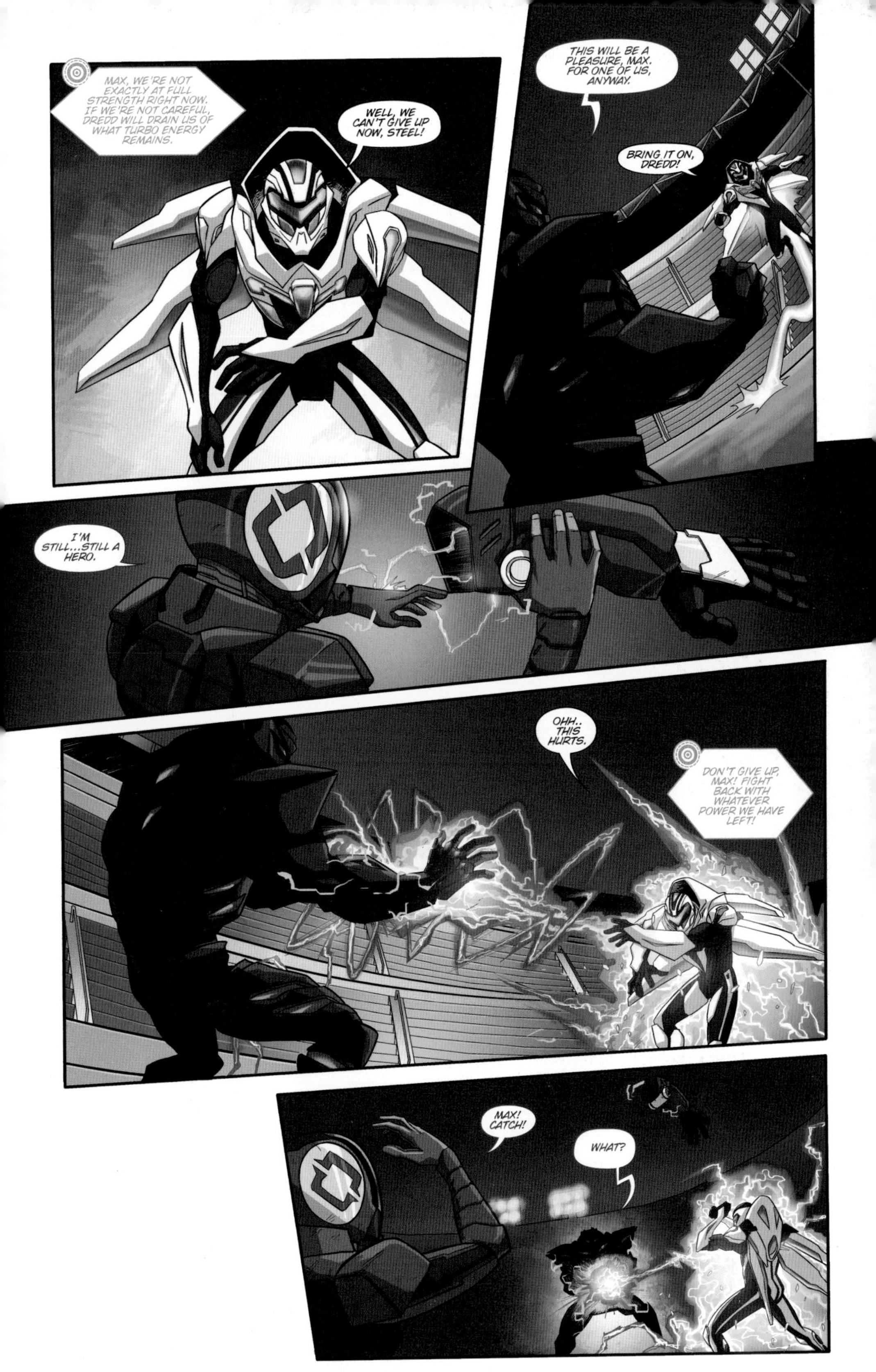
MAX, WE'RE NOT EXACTLY AT FULL STRENGTH RIGHT NOW. IF WE'RE NOT CAREFUL, DREDD WILL DRAIN US OF WHAT TURBO ENERGY REMAINS.
WELL, WE CAN'T GIVE UP NOW, STEEL!
THIS WILL BE A PLEASURE, MAX. FOR ONE OF US, ANYWAY.
BRING IT ON, DREDD!
I'M STILL...STILL A HERO.
OHH.. THIS HURTS.
DON'T GIVE UP, MAX! FIGHT BACK WITH WHATEVER POWER WE HAVE LEFT!
MAX! CATCH!
WHAT?

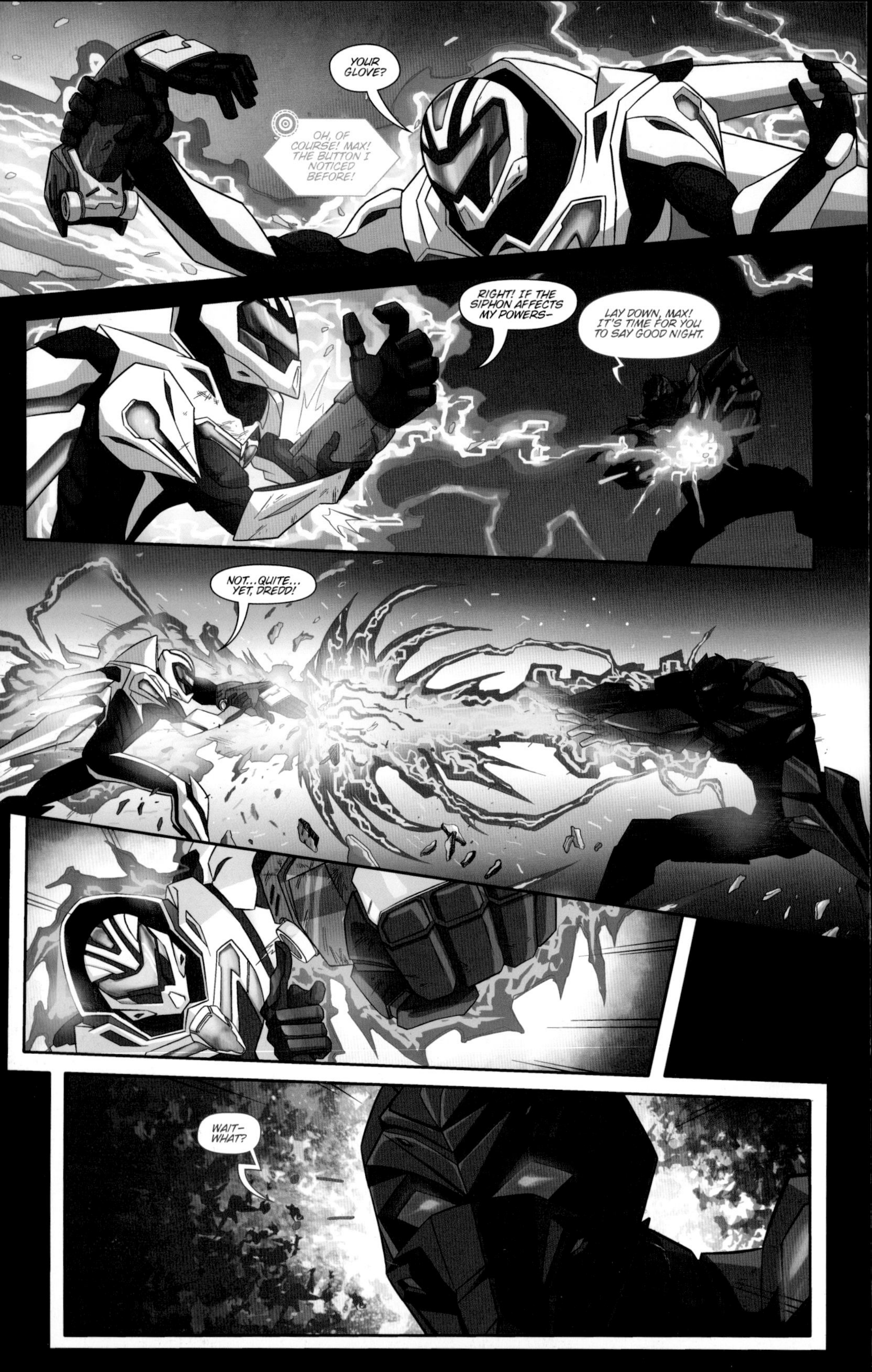
YOUR GLOVE?
OH, OF COURSE! MAX! THE BUTTON I NOTICED BEFORE!
RIGHT! IF THE SIPHON AFFECTS MY POWERS-
LAY DOWN, MAX! IT'S TIME FOR YOU TO SAY GOOD NIGHT.
NOT...QUITE... YET, DREDD!
WAIT- WHAT?

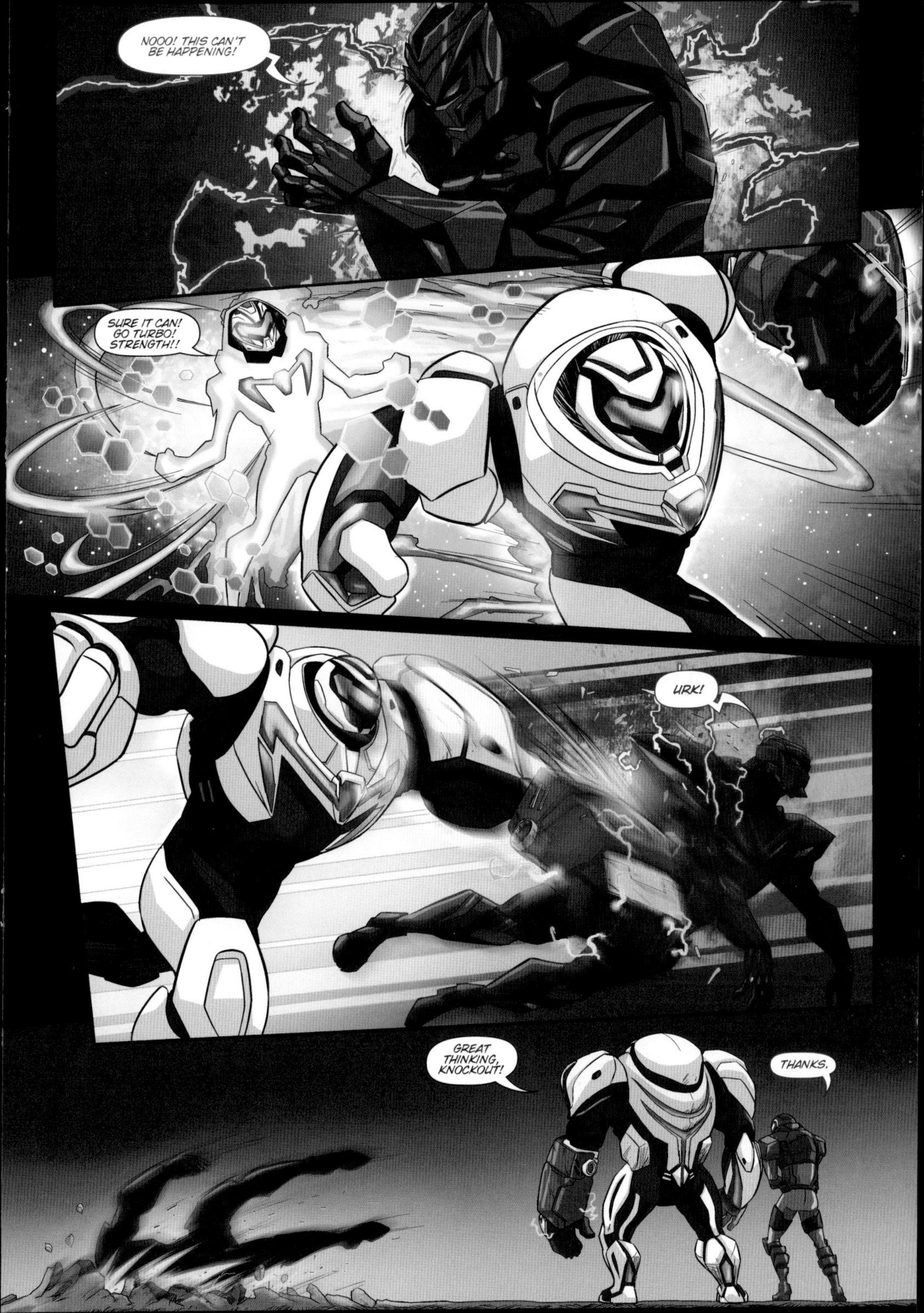
NOOO! THIS CAN'T BE HAPPENING!
SURE IT CAN! GO TURBO! STRENGTH!!
URK!
GREAT THINKING, KNOCKOUT!
THANKS.

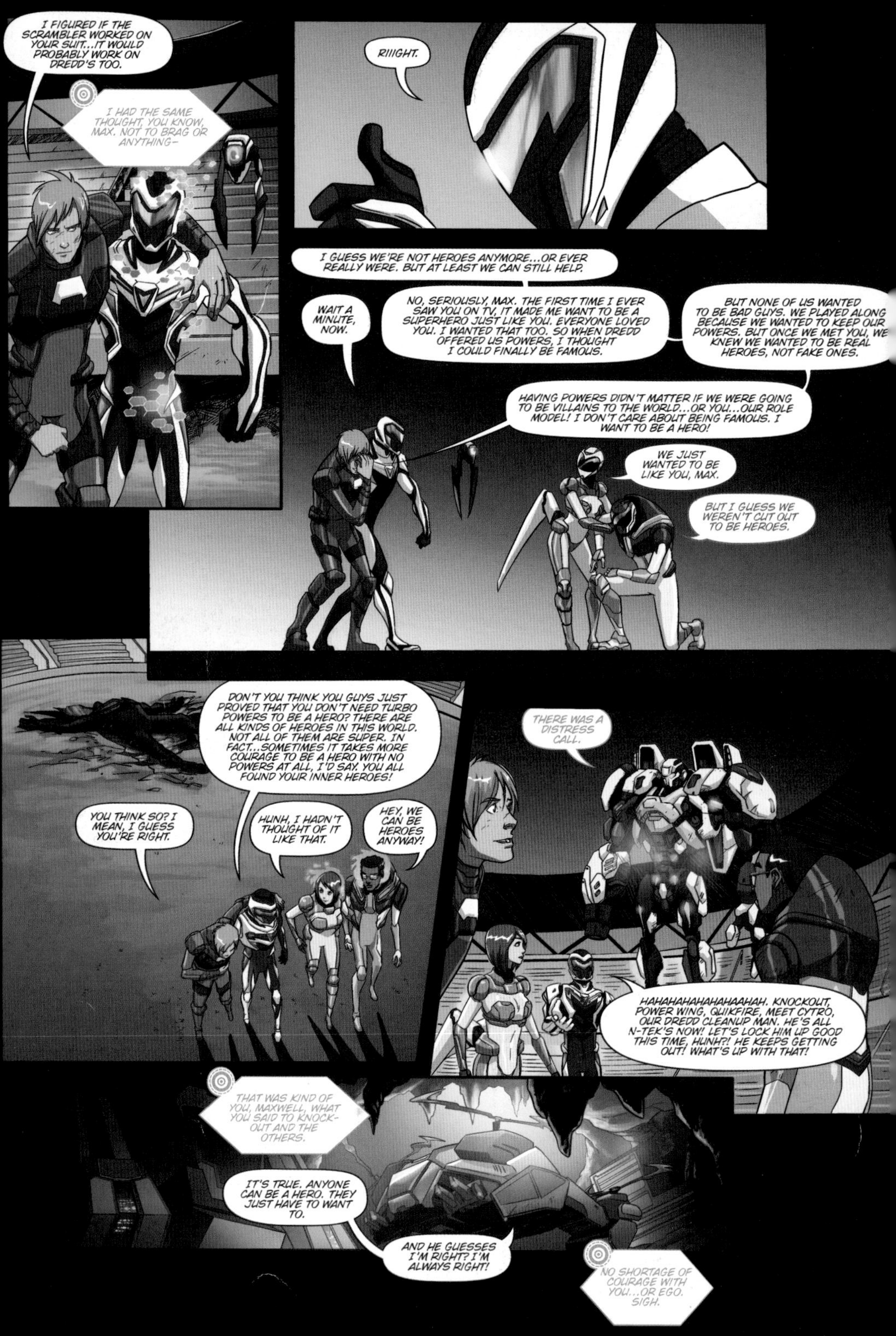
I FIGURED IF THE SCRAMBLER WORKED ON YOUR SUIT...IT WOULD PROBABLY WORK ON DREDD'S TOO.
I HAD THE SAME THOUGHT, YOU KNOW, MAX. NOT TO BRAG OR ANYTHING–
RIIIGHT.
I GUESS WE'RE NOT HEROES ANYMORE...OR EVER REALLY WERE. BUT AT LEAST WE CAN STILL HELP.
WAIT A MINUTE, NOW.
NO, SERIOUSLY, MAX. THE FIRST TIME I EVER SAW YOU ON TV, IT MADE ME WANT TO BE A SUPERHERO JUST LIKE YOU. EVERYONE LOVED YOU. I WANTED THAT TOO. SO WHEN DREDD OFFERED US POWERS, I THOUGHT I COULD FINALLY BE FAMOUS.
BUT NONE OF US WANTED TO BE BAD GUYS. WE PLAYED ALONG BECAUSE WE WANTED TO KEEP OUR POWERS. BUT ONCE WE MET YOU, WE KNEW WE WANTED TO BE REAL HEROES, NOT FAKE ONES.
HAVING POWERS DIDN'T MATTER IF WE WERE GOING TO BE VILLAINS TO THE WORLD...OR YOU...OUR ROLE MODEL! I DON'T CARE ABOUT BEING FAMOUS. I WANT TO BE A HERO!
WE JUST WANTED TO BE LIKE YOU, MAX.
BUT I GUESS WE WEREN'T CUT OUT TO BE HEROES.
DON'T YOU THINK YOU GUYS JUST PROVED THAT YOU DON'T NEED TURBO POWERS TO BE A HERO? THERE ARE ALL KINDS OF HEROES IN THIS WORLD. NOT ALL OF THEM ARE SUPER. IN FACT...SOMETIMES IT TAKES MORE COURAGE TO BE A HERO WITH NO POWERS AT ALL, I'D SAY. YOU ALL FOUND YOUR INNER HEROES!
YOU THINK SO? I MEAN, I GUESS YOU'RE RIGHT.
HUNH, I HADN'T THOUGHT OF IT LIKE THAT.
HEY, WE CAN BE HEROES ANYWAY!
THERE WAS A DISTRESS CALL.
HAHAHAHAHAHAHAHAAH. KNOCKOUT, POWER WING, QUIKFIRE, MEET CYTRO, OUR DREDD CLEANUP MAN. HE'S ALL N-TEK'S NOW! LET'S LOCK HIM UP GOOD THIS TIME, HUNH?! HE KEEPS GETTING OUT! WHAT'S UP WITH THAT!
THAT WAS KIND OF YOU, MAXWELL, WHAT YOU SAID TO KNOCK-OUT AND THE OTHERS.
IT'S TRUE. ANYONE CAN BE A HERO. THEY JUST HAVE TO WANT TO.
AND HE GUESSES I'M RIGHT? I'M ALWAYS RIGHT!
NO SHORTAGE OF COURAGE WITH YOU...OR EGO. SIGH.

B. CLAY MOORE has written comic books for virtually every major publisher, including Image Comics, Marvel Comics, DC Comics, WildStorm, Oni Press and Top Cow Productions. He is the co-creator of a handful of critically acclaimed creator-owned books.

COVER ARTIST

ALBERT CARRERES has worked on several comic and manga titles, including *Hand7*, a manga series published by Humanoïdes Associés, the Spanish comic book *Cálico Electronico*, the *Cars* movie prequel comic book, and two Marvel Comics projects featuring Iron Man and Antman. He was also the artist for *Voltron Force: Dragon Dawn* (VIZ Media).

COVER COLORS

ALEJANDRO TORRES is a comics artist who has worked for many publishers including Norma Editorial, Marvel Comics, Dark Horse – Sequential Pulp, IDW Publishing, Devil 's Due and VIZ Media, including doing colors on *Voltron Force: Dragon Dawn*.

ARTISTS - PAPILLON STUDIOS

(ART)

ALFA ROBBI was born and raised in Semarang City, Central Java, Indonesia. His published works include *Planetary Brigade* (Boom!) and *Ev* (TokyoPop). Robbi's current focus is Papillon, a comic book art studio he founded with Fajar Buana in 2002. Alfa was the illustrator for *Voltron Force: Rise of the Beast King* (VIZ Media).

(COLOR)

BURHAN ARIF was born in Semarang City, Central Java, Indonesia. He's an illustrator and colorist whose published works include *Ev* (TokyoPop), *Super Kaiju Hero Force* (Crispy) and *Voltron Force: Rise of the Beast King* (VIZ Media).

LETTERS

ZACK TURNER started out in the comics industry as an independent artist and as a colorist on *Unimaginable* (Arcana) and several projects for Bluewater. Recently he has been working on full art duties on *Redakai* (VIZ Media) and lettering *Monsuno* (VIZ Media).

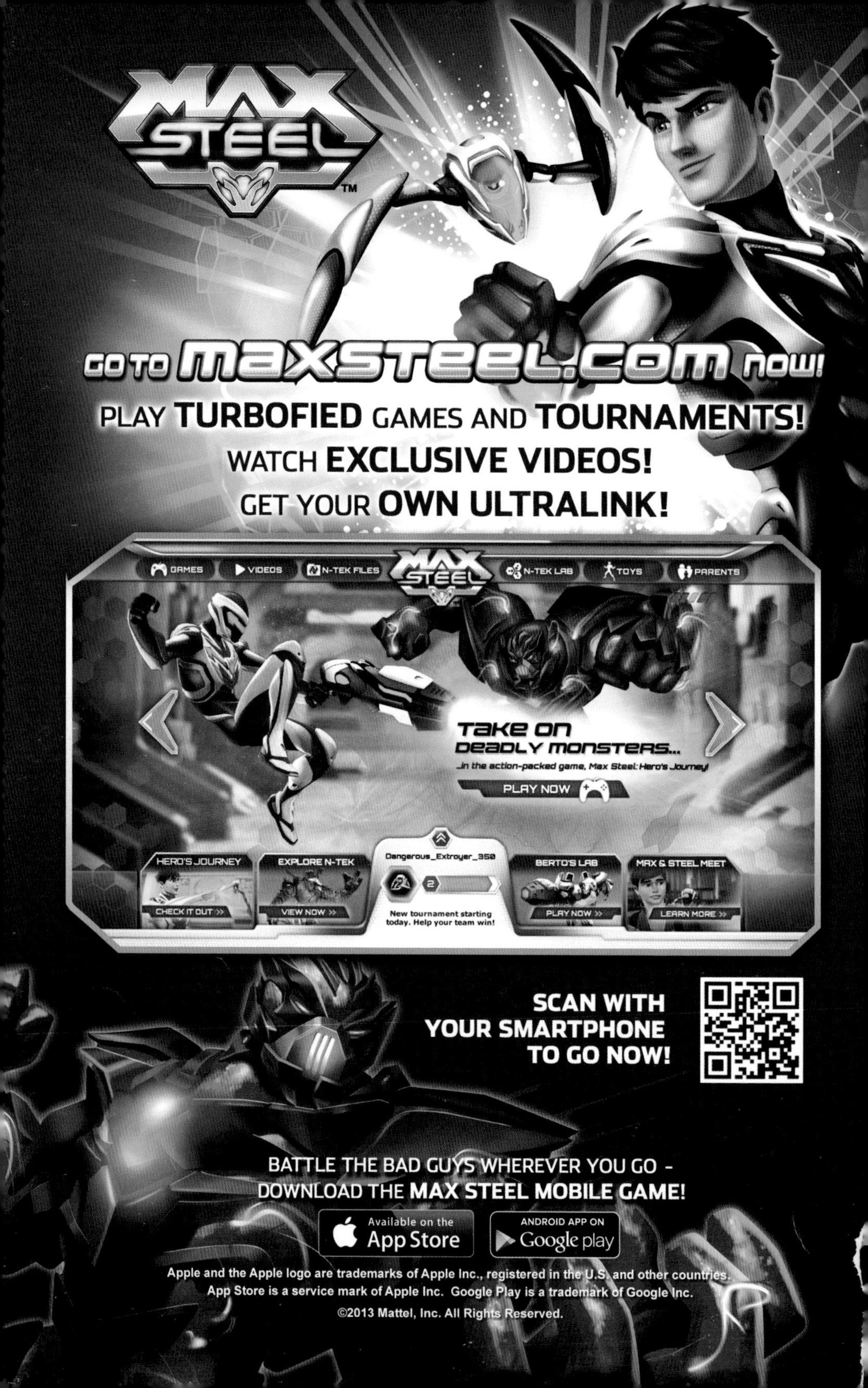
MAX STEEL™
GO TO MAXSTEEL.COM NOW!
PLAY TURBOFIED GAMES AND TOURNAMENTS!
WATCH EXCLUSIVE VIDEOS!
GET YOUR OWN ULTRALINK!
GAMES
VIDEOS
N-TEK FILES
MAX STEEL
N-TEK LAB
TOYS
PARENTS
TAKE ON DEADLY MONSTERS...
...in the action-packed game, Max Steel: Hero's Journey!
PLAY NOW
HERO'S JOURNEY
CHECK IT OUT »
EXPLORE N-TEK
VIEW NOW »
Dangerous_Extroyer_350
2
New tournament starting today. Help your team win!
BERTO'S LAB
PLAY NOW »
MAX & STEEL MEET
LEARN MORE »
SCAN WITH YOUR SMARTPHONE TO GO NOW!
BATTLE THE BAD GUYS WHEREVER YOU GO - DOWNLOAD THE MAX STEEL MOBILE GAME!
Available on the App Store
ANDROID APP ON Google play
Apple and the Apple logo are trademarks of Apple Inc., registered in the U.S. and other countries.
App Store is a service mark of Apple Inc. Google Play is a trademark of Google Inc.
©2013 Mattel, Inc. All Rights Reserved.